ORANGE PUBLIC LIBRARY

3 2159 00080 5305

P9-ELQ-682

ALSO BY CHARLOTTE AND AARON ELKINS:

A WICKED SLICE

BY AARON ELKINS

Gideon Oliver novels:

DEAD MEN'S HEARTS
MAKE NO BONES
ICY CLUTCHES
CURSES!
OLD BONES
MURDER IN THE QUEEN'S ARMES
THE DARK PLACE
FELLOWSHIP OF FEAR

Chris Norgren novels:

OLD SCORES
A GLANCING LIGHT
A DECEPTIVE CLARITY

Rotten Lies

Charlotte and Aaron
ELKINS

THE MYSTERIOUS PRESS

Published by Warner Books

A Time Warner Company

f/E
(mystery)

1995 B+T 1/96

Copyright © 1995 by Charlotte Elkins and Aaron J. Elkins
All rights reserved.

Mysterious Press books are published by Warner Books, Inc.,
1271 Avenue of the Americas, New York, NY 10020.

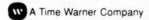 A Time Warner Company

The Mysterious Press name and logo are registered trademarks of Warner Books, Inc.

Printed in the United States of America

First printing: November 1995

10 9 8 7 6 5 4 3 2 1

Library of Congress Cataloging-in-Publication Data
Elkins, Charlotte.
    Rotten lies / Charlotte and Aaron Elkins.
        p. cm.
    ISBN 0-89296-598-3
    I. Elkins, Aaron J. II. Title.
PS3555.L485R6 1995
813'.54—dc20
                                                                            95-8462
                                                                            CIP

104611

Acknowledgments

As usual, a number of people have been generous with their help. We owe sincere thanks to:

-Don and Betty Hulbert of the Wing Point Golf and Country Club for introducing us to the intricacies of golf club administration.

-The Executive Women's Golf League, Seattle Chapter, and the Women's Club of the Meadowmeer Golf and Country Club, Bainbridge Island, for giving Charlotte so many opportunities for tournament play.

-Jerrod Hainline, Associate Producer, KIRO-TV, Seattle, for letting us get in his hair all during one particularly harrowing day of golf broadcasting.

-Sergeant John Chicoine of the Los Alamos, New Mexico, Police Department for filling us in on law enforcement matters in Los Alamos.

-Stephen Greenleaf, fellow mystery writer, for spending a summer of weekly golf outings with us in the fruitless hope of improving our play.

-Lawrence Vincent, M.D., another fellow mystery writer, for instructing us in the nature and effects of sports injuries.

Rotten Lies

Chapter 1

From his seat in the broadcast tower above the eighteenth green, Boyd Marriner watched the three vultures wheel slowly overhead, their outspread, fingerlike wing tips silhouetted black against a brilliant desert sky, as if expecting one of the players below them to drop dead at any moment.

Maybe they knew something he didn't, Boyd thought glumly. He almost hoped they did. Not that publicly expiring golfers were something to be wished for, but assuming that their allotted time was up anyway, and they were due to kick off in the near future in any case, would it hurt for them to do it—perhaps in the very act of missing their final earthly putt—under the rapt gaze of millions of television viewers?

Thousands, anyway. Two hours of Thursday afternoon women's golf was no match for Oprah or Geraldo under any circumstances, and this, the first day of the High Desert Classic, had been a dud from the word go. It wasn't that the play had been poor; it had been fairly good, as a matter of fact. But as associate producer of the American Sports Network's *Golf on Tour*, Boyd knew all too well that ratings didn't thrive on "fairly good" play. They needed absolutely wonderful play or—better yet—spectacularly lousy play, or anything but the deadly dull routine of one workmanlike stroke after another by one competent, sober pro after another.

Shielding his eyes against the glare he watched the dark birds float on the warm updrafts. More than he liked to admit, the damn things were bothering him. Not that he was superstitious, but vultures, notwithstanding all the crap about how they kept the desert nice and clean and sanitary, weren't what anybody would call good omens.

Still, he was toying with the idea of calling for a shot of them just to break the monotony, when Mike Bulger's voice, as stressed out as ever, came over his headset.

"Boyd, listen—Boyd, you there? Boyd?"

"Relax, Mike, I'm right here."

Mike was the executive producer, and he was calling from the "control truck"—the production trailer set up in its jungle of wires and cables in the staff parking area at the rear of the clubhouse, next to the dumpsters. Right there was one reason Boyd had never had any interest in an executive producer slot. Poor Mike would spend the entire four days of the tournament in a parking lot, rarely emerging from a stuffy, none-too-roomy trailer crammed with TV monitors and overambitious, hyperactive staff.

Boyd, on the other hand, had the best seat in the place, ten feet above the final green of the Cottonwood Creek golf course, a few feet away from Mary Ann Cooper and Skip Cochrane, the TV anchors. While Mike breathed secondhand air all day, Boyd sat up here on top of the world, in the fresh New Mexico breeze.

And watching buzzards for want of anything more exciting.

"Boyd, listen. Annette Hanson's on seventeen with two

straight birdies, just one stroke out of the lead. We need something on her."

"Right."

"And something's developing on the eleventh. One of the rabbits, Lee Ofsted, is coming on strong. Only three strokes out of the lead and starting to draw a gallery. She won't be in fixed-camera range until seventeen, but get some info ready just in case she stays hot. Which I doubt."

"Will do."

Mike's voice dropped a notch. "And pray that somebody screws up big-time or something pretty soon. This goddamn show's dying on its feet."

Boyd smiled. "I'll do that."

He riffled quickly through his box of five-by-eight-inch cards and passed Hanson's performance chart on to Skip Cochrane, who was doing color, then buzzed the graphics coordinator back in the control truck. "Ready with Hanson's career-win stats."

"Okey-doke."

Boyd turned his attention back to his cards and fished out a second one, not with any notable upsurge of hope.

Name: Lee Ofsted
Age: 23
Height: 5'9"
Weight: 130
Hometown: Portland, OR
Home club: North Portland Municipal Golf Course
College: AA Degree, U.S. Army, Continuing Ed.
Amateur record: None
Career Wins: None
Highest Finish: Eleventh, Pacific-Western Pro-Am
Last year's earnings: $17,000 (rookie year)
Position on the Money List: 98th
Exempt Status: Nonexempt

He scanned it a second time and leaned back in his canvas director's chair. Well, now. Could be there was something here after all. Ofsted was a "rabbit," all right, one of the horde of scrambling, usually young professional golfers so named because they survived (barely) by nibbling away at what was left of golf's green harvest after the stars had had their fill. Better yet, she wasn't one of your silver-spoon-in-the-mouth Ivy Leaguers with a string of collegiate titles either. How many others on the tour listed their highest degree as an AA from the Army's continuing education program? How many listed a public course as their home course?

Not many, that was for sure. And of those who did, they didn't very often show up on the leaderboard three strokes shy of the lead.

Which was why they were rabbits, of course.

And now a rabbit, an unheralded, self-made twenty-three-year-old, was fighting her way into contention at a major tournament. It could make a terrific story, just what he needed. Everybody would be pulling for her. He hoped she didn't fade. And he hoped she was pretty; that wouldn't hurt either. If she was able to stay on track for the final seven holes of the day—a big order—he would have the opening "tease" for tomorrow's telecast: "Don't bother turning on *Sports Tonight* for today's big headline. We've got the story right here and you won't want to miss it. An all-American, up-by-her-bootstraps story in the making . . ." Not bad. He took a dog-eared notepad from his shirt pocket and jotted it down.

One curious thing, though. Why was she playing prime time, along with the Torresdahls and the Hansons and the Kells? Ordinarily, first-day schedules called for the noncontenders to be out there either at the crack of dawn with the "dew sweepers" or in the waning afternoon light with the "litter brigade"; that is, long before or after broadcast time.

But here was Ofsted coming through right in the middle of the live TV coverage. How come?

It took a moment to punch in Bonnie Harlow's number on his cellular telephone and pose just that question. Bonnie was the field director of community relations of the Women's Professional Golf League, wandering somewhere on the course in her blue-and-white golf cart. He had long ago learned that if there was anything he needed to know about the WPGL and its mysterious workings, asking Bonnie was the quickest way to find out.

But not necessarily the most restful. "Oh, God, not now!" was her booming response, but then Bonnie was like that, always juggling twenty balls at the same time, always seemingly two steps away from implosion and disaster. But one way or another she generally got number twenty-one up in the air as well, like a never-say-die trained seal using both flippers, its tail, and its nose too—and even managed to seem as if she were having a jolly old time through it all.

He waited confidently.

"What?" he heard her say to someone else. *"What?"* A muffled, agitated, typically Bonnie-like conversation followed, and then her husky voice was on the phone once more.

"Boyd? What was it you wanted again? This better be life-or-death, pet."

He told her again.

"Yes, yes, yes, yes, yes. Just a minute, let me see who she's playing with." The handset was put down. Papers rustled mightily. There was a faint, abstracted "Damn, now where did I put that thing? Marjorie, lamb, have you seen my, my, what-do-you-call-it?"

Now what difference would it make who Ofsted was playing with, he wondered idly, while the fussing continued at the other end of the line. The first day of the Classic—Thursday—was structured as a pro-am: each foursome was composed of one woman professional golfer and three Cottonwood members who had paid heftily for the privilege of playing alongside a pro for the day. Friday's, Saturday's, and Sunday's rounds would be professional only, a dead-earnest competition for a purse of $500,000, but the scores the pros got today would count in the total. The amateurs, however, were hacking away just for the glory of it and for a variety of goofball prizes to be awarded at the pairings party tonight. As far as he knew, none of the play-alongs was a celebrity of any kind—this wasn't the old Crosby—so what difference did it make who Ofsted was playing with?

He listened to Bonnie shuffle paper and watched the buzzards. They were peeling off now and drifting away. A good sign?

"Oho, I have it!" she cried. "One of her partners is Peg Fiske, the tournament VIP in charge of corporate sponsorship."

"So?" said Boyd, when it appeared that this was her total answer.

"So she raised almost a million dollars, which means she can play with anybody she feels like, anytime she wants. And she wanted to be paired with Lee Ofsted. Don't ask me why, when you consider who else is playing. Maybe they're friends?"

"Is she pretty, do you know? Ofsted, I mean."

"Why? For Pete's sake, will you tell me what that has to do with anything?"

"I'm just doing my job, Bon. Is she pretty?"

Bonnie made an indecipherable noise, half-snort, half-laugh. "Well, my guess is someone like *you* would think she looks just great."

He didn't dare ask what that meant, but she was probably right. He was fifty-nine; not many twenty-three-year-olds were going to look anything but great to him. Still, some looked more great than others.

"Boyd, I'm up to my ears here. They're making me crazy. I've got a million things to do—"

He rang off and buzzed an assistant director in the control truck. "How's Ofsted doing?"

"Birdie the eleventh, eagle on the twelfth."

Well, now, this just might actually turn into something. He considered sending out someone with a handheld Mini-cam to tag along with her and get some extra footage to play with, but dismissed the idea. She wouldn't be used to that kind of attention and the pressure might make her choke, and that was the last thing they wanted to happen. Not when things were really starting to look up.

He leaned comfortably back in his chair, hands clasped behind his neck—only to feel a sudden shiver trickle slowly down his spine when a shadow drifted unexpectedly over the papers scattered on his sunlit table. He looked up.

Overhead, the buzzards were back.

Chapter 2

The view from the tee at the sixteenth hole was enough to take your breath away: a lush sweep of fairway green snaking between dry, pinyon-studded hills, with hazy purple tablelands beyond, and all of it in the shadow of the looming Jemez Mountains. Lee Ofsted saw none of it: only a tight 430-yard par-5 with a tricky dogleg to the left and a green that was faster than she liked.

She held out her hand. "Driver," she said to her caddie.

"Well, of course, driver," Lou grumbled. "What'd you think I was gonna give you, a putter?"

She smiled. "Sorry, Lou," she said, watching him mutteringly pull the protective sock off the club.

He was right to be offended. Nine times out of ten he knew which club she needed before she did. Lou was a gruff, funny little guy almost a head shorter than she was and well over twice her age; as rough, and gnarled, and knotted as an old apple tree. And just as sturdy and dependable. He'd been with her, whenever she could get him, almost her entire professional career.

Over a year now.

"Go for it," he said, handing her the wood. He tilted his head to peer encouragingly up at her. "Why screw around?"

She nodded, her eyes on the fairway. An eddy in the breeze carried a fragment of conversation from the gallery gathered behind the rope to the right of the tee.

"Why, that's a beat-up old persimmon club she's got. Anybody would think a pro like that would be using *metal* woods these days."

Lee smiled to herself. Yes, anybody would think so, all right. Anybody would also think "a pro like that" could afford a new set of clubs anytime she wanted one. That just showed how much anybody knew. Most pros never paid for their equipment at all, they got it free from promotion-savvy sporting good companies. The only ones who didn't get free clubs were the only ones who needed them: the rabbits. Well, maybe, if she could keep up anything like the level of play she'd been at for the last five holes, she *would* be replacing this hand-me-down set of hers after Saturday. Yes, with metal woods.

Metal woods, she thought absently. Now there was a funny term for you. There was a name for expressions like that—moroxyn . . . oxormyon . . .

She jerked her head irritably. Her concentration was slipping; that meant she was wearing down, easing off. And she couldn't let that happen. Not today, not when she was playing the best golf of her life. For the first time there was a sizable—and respectful—gallery chugging along with her over the course. For the first time her partners, even her generally unimpressible friend Peg Fiske, were treating her with something between diffidence and awe.

And for the first time, the first, sweet, thrilling, utterly terrifying time, she had a chance to finish the opening day of a tournament in the lead. Three holes to go. If she could keep her focus, keep the easy, confident rhythm she'd gotten going, she knew she could do it. But the seventeenth, that was the worrisome one; she'd been vacillating over that one all day . . .

Easy, she told herself. Hold it, there you go again. You can only play 'em one at time, as Lou had been growling at her all day. And sixteen came before seventeen.

She wiped sweat from her forehead, looking out over the fairway toward the flag, hidden by the crook of the dogleg. The tee box, where she was standing, was on a small bluff perhaps thirty feet high. From there her drive would have to cross a rock-littered ravine about 150 yards out—the Crack of Doom, Peg had called it on their practice round. Cottonwood was her home course and Peg maintained that the ravine was paved three feet deep with golf balls, most of them put there by her.

But while that gulch might give the heebie-jeebies to the Pegs of this world, Lee hardly gave it a thought. A pro who had to worry about clearing a hazard 150 yards out wouldn't be a pro for very long.

No, Lee had something else to worry about. Cottonwood was a brilliantly designed course, with heebie-jeebies for the scratch players as well as the duffers. On the sixteenth, the difficulty was strategic. Just before the fairway twisted sharply to the left, skirting a string of lavish fairway homes, an extensive, reed-choked pond sat smack in the landing area about 230 yards from the tee, taking up three-quarters of the fairway width and extending well into the rough on the right.

If you wanted to play it safe and settle for par there was no problem: a 190- or 200-yard drive down the left side with a long iron would bring you up safely short of the pond, from where another long iron would take you through the gap and past the dogleg to within 50 yards of the green. A chip shot, two putts, and you were in. Five strokes total; par.

But if you didn't want to settle for par, then you had to

gamble. In this case, the gamble was a knee-knocker; a controlled hook, a big all-out drive with enough sidespin to bend its flight and send it in a long arc that tailed off to the left, matching the curve of the dogleg and landing the ball well beyond the water, leaving only a single medium-iron shot to the green. Two putts, and there you were with a four—a birdie.

The problem lay with that "controlled" hook, a euphemism if ever there was one. Hooks were about as controllable as mine explosions; the best of pros had trouble putting them where they wanted them. And in this case an uncontrolled hook was going to come down out of bounds—that would mean a penalty—in one of the backyards along the left side of the fairway. Last year in Houston she had hooked a fairway shot into somebody's swimming pool. During a poolside barbecue. They had very civilly offered her a hot dog and a drink. She had turned down the drink, but inasmuch as she was hopelessly out of contention by then anyway, she had accepted the hot dog. It was delicious, but it hadn't helped her game; she had finished the day with an 80, not even making the cut.

But today she was most definitely in contention, and a stroke-and-distance penalty . . .

No, best not to think about it. Lee wasn't much for playing it safe even when it was the wisest course (which was most of the time, especially for someone whose all-time big day had been an eleventh-place finish the previous year). Lou wasn't much for them either. She knew perfectly well what his "Go for it" had meant.

She stepped up to the ball and took her stance. A final glance down the fairway. A single, concise waggle of the club. A shallow, nervous breath, taken in and let out through her mouth. A brief shutting of her eyes to blot out everything else.

Now. Ground the club. Sweep it slowly back. Coil, coil . . .

And swing.

* * *

Boyd sat stiffly upright, pressing the headphones to his ears, intent on the audio portion of the telecast. For a moment he held his breath, then whacked the cluttered table with his palm. By God, she'd done it, a birdie on sixteen! Ofsted had moxie, all right. Not only had she snatched the lead, but she was closing in on the course's single-day record— Did she know that? he wondered—and she'd done it on sheer guts. To his surprise, he realized that he was actually rooting for her. Not merely because it would make good television, but because he wanted to see her win. It was nice to know he could still regress to being a golf fan after all these years. Once in a while, anyway.

Well, the make-or-break test would come now, on the seventeenth, a par-4 hole that had been giving everyone fits. Seventeen was straight as an arrow—no problem there— and only 260 yards, a seemingly undemanding par-4, complicated only by a nasty outcropping of pinyon that jutted well out into the fairway from the left-hand rough just short of the green, blocking anything like a direct approach to it. Still, under ordinary circumstances, a competent golfer would have no trouble with it. A 230-yard drive to put the ball beside or just short of the outcropping, then chip or lob up to the green, and you were home free.

But today, in this thin, mile-high air, the pros were getting more distance than they were used to, and that was creating temptations for the bolder ones. A little extra oomph, a little more loft, and a well-hit ball just might clear the outcropping altogether and make it all the way to the green. In one stroke.

Four of the pros had tried it. One had made it and two-putted for a triumphant birdie. The other three had landed in the rocky tangle of vegetation, countryside better suited to hunting mountain lions than golf balls, and had deconstructed—that had been Skip's rather apt word for it—in a nightmare of unplayable lies, lost balls, penalty strokes, and muffed shots. One had taken an eight on the hole, and all three were now hopelessly out of contention.

Last night in the bar at the Hilltop House, he had heard a group of professionals sitting over their drinks and shaking their heads after their practice rounds, endlessly discussing seventeen, worrying about how to handle it when it counted. Pros did a lot of that, rehashing golf holes the way old generals talked about distant battlefields: the immense, sandy wastes of the third at Pine Valley, the treacherous, undulating tenth green at Winged Foot, the tear-drenched bunkers known as the Beardies that line the fourteenth at venerable St. Andrews.

Come to think of it, something like that might make a good short feature on Saturday, maybe starting with the seventeenth here, then segueing into a humorous piece: famous players blowing it on famous holes. Get a little film footage from the library. Then wind up back on Cottonwood's seventeenth—the do-or-die hole.

The notepad came out of his pocket again for a few quick scratches and Boyd turned his attention back to the audio on his headset. They had just finished describing Kell's 22-foot putt on the twelfth and were back to Lee Ofsted, who was now teeing up on seventeen herself.

"They," of course, were Skip and Mary Ann, doing color commentary and play-by-play respectively, sitting under the awning a few feet from him and calling the action by means of the monitors on their table. Boyd slid his chair around for his own first look at Lee Ofsted, a mid-distance shot from the tee box camera.

Well, now, she did look great, he thought appreciatively.

Pretty, blonde, graceful, leggy—svelte, in fact; nothing like the pug-nosed, wiry street urchin he'd dreamed up. That was good: the scrambling young pro from the other side of the tracks who looked—and moved—like Grace Kelly. Or close enough for the American Sports Network.

"My guess is she's going to go for it, Skip," Mary Ann's serious, earnest voice said four feet away from him, and directly into his ear through the headset. "She's got that look on her face."

"I'd say you're right, Mary Ann. That's been this spunky twenty-three-year-old's attitude all day. Spunk, spunk, and more spunk. And it certainly hasn't done her any harm, has it, Mary Ann?"

"No, it certainly hasn't, Skip. A birdie here will just about put her out of reach for the round."

"And what a thrill that would be for this unknown young golfer from Portland, Oregon, way down at ninety-eighth place on the money list. What do you think, Mary Ann, does she have a chance?"

"Well, if it was me, I wouldn't try it, but Lee hits a little further off the tee than I ever did. Not that much further, though," she added ominously.

Boyd watched Ofsted's club sweep evenly, almost casually back, listened to the soul-satisfying click of clubhead against ball, and watched it soar, white against a deep blue sky (the contrast expertly enhanced by the engineer fiddling with his dials in the truck).

"It's a beautiful drive, Mary Ann!" exclaimed Skip, the more histrionic of the two.

"No-o-o, I don't think so . . ."

"I think it's going to clear . . ."

"No-o-o, I don't think so . . ."

"*Get up there, you bugger!*" a third voice said, urgent and hoarse. Boyd smiled. That was the field mike picking up Lou Somebody, Ofsted's hoary old codger of a caddie, a rare holdover from the days when caddies didn't have BAs. Or grade-school diplomas.

"It's going to clear . . . !" Skip cried, shouting now. He was up off his chair an inch or two. "It's going to make it, she—she—" Abruptly he sagged back onto the canvas seat. "Oh, good golly, Miss Molly."

"No," said Mary Ann, just a little smugly. "I didn't think so. She's in the rough on seventeen—the latest in a long parade today."

"So Lee Ofsted's spunk has finally cost her here on the infamous seventeenth," a sad Skip Cochrane intoned into his microphone.

It damn sure had, Boyd thought bleakly. Scratch Ofsted for tomorrow's tease, she was out of it. Try that do-or-die feature instead. Too bad, it'd be a lot more work. And too bad about her too.

"Shit," Mike Bulger's voice crackled into his ear.

"Well, hello to you too," Boyd said pleasantly. "How are things with you?"

But levity wasn't Mike's forte. "Did you see? There goes our human interest."

"I saw."

"Well, the hell with it, we'll come up with something else. Maybe some kind of a . . ." The pause indicated a Mike Bulger brainstorm in the making. "Hey, about a piece on, you know, disaster holes in general? Bobby Locke's eight on the fourteenth at St. Andrews, Dale Douglass's nineteen on whatever the hell hole it was at Pebble Beach? And now the seventeenth at Cottonwood? What do you think, is that a great idea or what?"

Boyd sighed. "It's a great idea, Mike. Sure wish I'd thought of it."

"Okay, see what you can do. And listen, is that lightning feature ready? The one the club liaison—the jerk—swore we'd never need this late in the season?"

"It's in the can. Four minutes, forty-five seconds."

"Good, the weather report says there are going to be thunderstorms in the mountains tomorrow. If we have to close down play, we'll show it. And fill in with interviews if we have to, God help us."

Boyd groaned. Goodbye ratings, or what was left of them. "Don't tell me these things, Mike, I don't want to know."

Chapter 3

Lee's ball was in a better position than she deserved. On its way to skipping out of bounds it had been saved by the low stone wall that served as the boundary marker. Moreover, it lay on an open, relatively level patch of hardpan, not buried in a bush or sunk in a gully, as she had feared. Better yet, with the flag placed as it was on the left side of the green, the hole was only 20 yards away. And best of all, the route that the ball would take to get there was blocked only by some stunted juniper that could easily be cleared with a soft, lofted stroke, a simple, easy pitch.

But.

Apparently the ball had bounced off the wall, gone partially up a sandy hummock, then rolled back down to come to rest only sixteen inches from the wall itself. If she wanted to shoot toward the hole, in other words, she would have to do it standing on top of a two-foot-high stone wall. Or straddling it. With a total of sixteen inches for her backswing. Make that fourteen inches, once you allowed for the breadth of the clubhead.

Lee's stomach had turned over when she saw it. So, judging

from her expression, did Peg's. "Lee, you're not going to try it!" she exclaimed when she heard her ask Lou for her 9-iron. Peg had taken her usual four strokes to get to the green and had come back to offer sympathy and condolences to her friend.

"Of course I am, Peg," Lee said in what she hoped was a voice of serene confidence. She did not feel serene. She certainly didn't feel confident. She wasn't sure that what she had in mind could be done.

Peg, never one to hide her feelings, was transparently dismayed. "But you can't! It's impossible! There isn't— Lee, please be sensible, declare an unplayable lie. *Take* a lousy penalty stroke, you'll still be tied for the lead and tomorrow's another day. Nobody—"

"Lady, give it a rest," Lou said severely. "My golfer's trying to take her shot."

Properly chagrined, Peg gave it a rest and dropped back twenty feet.

Lee looked at her caddie. "Well, what do you think, Lou? Is it possible?"

He thought about it, then scowled gloomily up at her. "It ain't probable."

In his place she would have been glum too; in his mind's eye he was probably watching the shriveling of his 6 percent share of her prize money. Had he known what she was contemplating, Lee thought, he would have been glummer still.

For Lee was not going to shoot for the hole by standing on the wall, or by straddling it, or by draping her body across it. She wasn't going to shoot for the hole at all; not directly. She was going in the opposite direction. She was going to hit the ball *into* the wall, to ricochet it off the stone the way a pool player would hit a carom shot off a side cushion. If all went well, it would bounce back over her head and onto the green.

In 1976, in a similar situation at the Phoenix Open, Tom Watson had tried the same thing. And it had paid off.

She made a couple of abbreviated practice swings and took her stance, hearing a murmur of surprise from her much-diminished gallery when they saw her facing in the wrong direction. Well, no wonder. She was no Tom Watson; she knew that even better than they did. And what she was doing was replete with potential catastrophe. She barely knew how to play pool. What did she know about caroms? What if she misjudged the angle, which seemed highly likely? Or what if she popped the ball *over* the wall, directly out of bounds? What if the ball came back and hit *her*? That would be a two-stroke penalty. What if it hit her and then bounced back over the wall and out of bounds? That would cost her *another* two strokes. And make her look like an utter klutz, but that was the least of her worries.

Momentarily, she wavered. The nearby presence of the cameraman, who had repositioned himself when he realized (with a muttered four-letter exclamation of disbelief) what she was going to do, didn't help either. Being filmed didn't mean she was on television at the moment, of course. With over a dozen cameras on the course grinding away at the same time, a golfer had no way of knowing what was on the air at any given moment. But she knew that a circus shot like this couldn't fail to show up on the sports highlights programs that night. And if she did actually manage to bounce the ball off her own noggin, then she was assured of a place of honor in every sports-bloopers video of the next twenty years.

Fame at last.

Still, there she was just 20 yards from the pin, and the idea of meekly throwing in the towel and declaring an unplayable lie went against her grain. A birdie was out of the question now, but if she could ricochet the ball onto the green she still had a chance at par.

She gripped down on the club, focused her mind, lectured herself. You can do this, Lee. Weight on the left leg. Hit down on the ball to get it up in the air. Don't worry about the precise direction; all you're trying to do is get it *anywhere* on the eight hundred square feet of the green. And, above all, no follow-through. The worst possible thing she could do would be to slam the clubhead into the wall and wind up injuring her wrist or arm.

Her short, choppy stroke clipped the ball sharply off the stone wall, bringing a gasp from those people in the crowd who hadn't yet figured out what she was intending. She knew at once that she had struck it too hard and spun around, her heart sinking as she saw it sail twenty feet higher and thirty feet farther than she intended, over the flag to the far apron of the green. But she had also put more backspin on it than she meant to and she watched with astonishment as it hopped drunkenly backward and trickled to a stop three feet from the hole—*three feet*—bringing another gasp from the crowd, followed by a cheer.

She raised her club and smiled graciously to acknowledge them, just as if she wasn't as flabbergasted as anybody else. As she did, she got her first hint of something wrong, a twinge in the upper part of her left forearm as she lifted the club. No more than a minor twinge, but worrisome all the same. Had she pulled up on her follow-through too abruptly and sprained something? Had she driven her club too forcefully into the hardpan on her downswing? Nervously, she kneaded her forearm. No, it felt all right, nothing serious, just another passing ache. During the tour season it was a rare time when there wasn't some part of her that hurt.

Five minutes later, after her partners had holed out with a five, a six, and an eight (Peg), Lee sank the putt. Amazingly, she had her birdie after all, and she followed it with a conservatively played par on the final hole. She was shaking as she picked up the ball; the adrenaline crash she'd held off by sheer willpower until she finished the round had finally come. And she was strangely close to tears. Unless somebody following her had an even more extraordinary round than she'd had, she would be the first-day leader, with a better score than golfers she still regarded with something like hero worship, golfers whose mere presence was enough to make her tongue-tied and shy. And one of the marshals had told her that her 64 was a Cottonwood record.

It was certainly an Ofsted record.

It was bewildering, too much to take in. She turned to leave the green feeling more dazed than happy. When the crowd, always largest at the eighteenth green, showered her with warm applause it took a few seconds for her to react. Again she waved to them, this time with her putter.

And again she felt the twinge, more intense this time, hotter, sharper, a stab of unfamiliar pain. Until now she had been luckier than most; never had she had an injury serious enough to keep her from playing even for a single day.

She shut her eyes and massaged her arm. Please, God, not now of all times, not this tournament. Not now.

Chapter 4

But Lee had never been able to stay downbeat for long. By the time she had walked with Peg to the scoring tent, hearing congratulations from every side (a delightful new experience), she had convinced herself that divine intervention was unnecessary, that a couple of aspirin now, and maybe two more when she went to bed, would take care of everything.

Inside the green-and-white tent, she sat down at one of the folding tables to make sure her scorecard was accurate and countersign it before turning it in and making it official.

"Take your time," Peg told her. "Now is not the moment to screw up."

Lee nodded happily. Peg didn't have to tell her to take her time. The last thing she wanted to do was rush this. If they would let her, she'd be perfectly content to sit there for the rest of the day and simply look at those wonderful numbers. They were amazing, incredible . . . a *three* on the twelfth, a *four* on the sixteenth—my God, she'd taken chances! And when she thought about that carom on seventeen . . . Where had she found the nerve . . .

Her stomach twisted all over again. Gulping, she signed the card and handed it in before some grim-faced WPGL official found her and told her that her score wouldn't count because she didn't deserve it; she'd been too lucky. And too foolhardy.

"What you need to do first," Peg said soberly as they stepped back into the harsh midafternoon sun, "is have a doctor look at that arm."

"What I need to do first," Lee told her, is "eat a giant cheeseburger with all the trimmings. Bacon, even. And a large order of fries. And a strawberry milkshake."

"Well, then, second," Peg allowed. "You do look like you could use something to eat." She brightened. "And I could stand a bite myself. Let's go to the clubhouse snack bar. We can eat out on the deck and watch the rest of the field come in."

Thirty minutes later, under a Bavarian beer umbrella, a much-restored, much-relaxed Lee finished the last of her fries and gulped what was left of her melted milkshake.

"I remember when I used to be able to eat like that," said a wistful Peg, who had eaten exactly the same thing Lee had, with the exception of leaving over an inch-square wedge of hamburger and two bedraggled French fries.

"Let's have some tea or coffee or something and stay out here a little longer," Lee suggested. "There are still half a dozen foursomes to come in."

Peg shook her head. "Will you stop worrying? There's nobody out there who can catch you, not in a million years."

"Who's worrying?" Lee said. "I'm gloating. This is sheer bliss."

"A sixty-four," Peg said reverently. "I still can't believe it. Is that the best score you've ever made in a tournament?"

Lee laughed. "By a mile." In a tournament or out of it. "Everything came together today. My fade was working,

23

my draw was working, my putting was working—for a change—and my chips were right on target. Everything."

"You were also damned lucky."

Lee eyed her gravely, then looked around as if to make sure no one could overhear. "Was I ever," she whispered, and they both burst into laughter.

There were not many people with whom she felt as much at ease, as free to be candid, as she did with this plump, bluff middle-aged woman with a voice like a tuba. Lee and Peg Fiske had been randomly teamed at a pro-am the previous year and had hit it off at once despite a twenty-year difference in age, a $250,000-or-thereabouts disparity in net annual income, and a total nonintersection of social circles. Peg's father had been a psychiatrist, her mother a professor. Her husband, Ric, was a research physicist and she herself was president and CEO of a management consulting firm. They lived, Lee knew, in a five-thousand-square-foot Santa Fe—style home on the first fairway here at Cottonwood Creek.

Lee's father laid cement for a living. Her mother had never had a job other than housewife and mother. They still lived where Lee and her five brothers and sisters had been born, in a 1950s wood-frame house in Gresham, Oregon, with a linoleum-floored front porch and a crabgrass yard. "If it's green, mow it," was her father's philosophy of lawn care. Lee herself lived in a nondescript two-room apartment in Portland's Sellwood district. When she was on the tour, which was most of the time, she generally took a room in a Motel 6 or a Super 8, whichever was closest to the course. When she was in a financial bind, which was pretty often, she even shared a room with another rabbit, something she hated.

And her boyfriend, if that's what Graham still was, was a cop.

And yet the two women had quickly become friends,

24

although the WPGL tour schedule made it difficult for Lee to see Peg very often. Or anyone else, for that matter. She hadn't seen her family in three months. She hadn't seen Graham in . . . but that was a different story . . .

"Harry Harrelson, that's who you'll see," Peg said abruptly, when they'd brought their coffee back to their table.

Lee returned from a long way away. "Come again?"

"About your arm. Harry's—"

Lee waved her off. "Peg, it's just a twinge. It already feels better, honestly. I don't know what I was making such a fuss about."

But Peg wasn't that easy to put off. "Harry's an orthopedic surgeon, absolutely crackerjack, and a golfer too. He's on our board."

"An orthopedic surgeon? For this?" She waggled her arm. "You've got to be kidding. He'd laugh me out of his office." And put her budget into cardiac arrest.

"If it's money you're worried about—"

"Peg, don't start," Lee said warningly.

"Relax, I'm not offering to pay. But Harry owes me megafavors and he'd be more than willing—"

"No, really, Peg. Believe me, if I thought I'd seriously hurt something, I wouldn't hesitate."

"Like heck you wouldn't," Peg said. "You're afraid to have a doctor look at it because you're scared to death you'll be told you shouldn't play the rest of the tournament, and you don't want that to happen. You'd rather pretend everything's okay and play through, and *then* see a doctor— maybe when it's too late and you've done yourself some permanent damage."

Peg swigged aggressively at her glass. "Am I right, or am I right?"

Lee smiled. "I guess you're right."

"And is that crazy, or is that crazy?"

"All right, you win," Lee said. "I'll see somebody. But I don't need an orthopedic surgeon. The WPGL has a trainer that comes along on the tour. He's around here somewhere. I'll go talk to him."

"Well, all right, then," Peg said sternly. "Honestly." Then she softened. "Lee, you really do look beat. You ought to get yourself some rest too." The fanny pack on Peg's midriff began emitting muted sounds. "What now?" she muttered, unzipping it and pulling out her cellular phone.

"Yes . . .? You're kidding, lightning this late in the season . . .? He *what?*" Peg's eyes rolled upward. "Doesn't Vernon know it's not up to us? It's completely up to the WPGL officials. Look, can't you just sit down with him and explain . . ." For a moment she listened, shaking her head, then sighed. "I know, tell me about it. Well, see if you can get hold of Bonnie and ask her to come and explain it to him. And I'll be there in a jiff. 'Bye."

She folded the telephone with a wry smile and stowed it away. "One of our board members—the chairman of the rules committee, no less—doesn't quite understand the rules. He's called a meeting to talk about criteria for canceling play if we get lightning tomorrow." She glanced sharply at Lee. "God forbid."

"Amen," Lee said. "I'll second that."

"Now where were we? I was giving you some invaluable advice, no doubt."

"You were telling me to get some rest."

"Oh, yeah. Well, do."

"I will. Look, would it be awful of me if I didn't show up at the pairings party tonight? I think maybe I ought to crawl into bed by seven or so and stay there. It's another big day tomorrow."

"Sure, good idea. I'll make excuses for you, don't worry about it. Now go find that trainer, or do I have to drag you myself?"

Lee crushed her straw into the empty glass and stood up. "I'm on my way."

* * *

"It's tennis elbow, is what it is."

Lee stared at the pleasant, moon-faced young man who had spent the last ten minutes poking and twisting her left forearm and asking question after question, usually variations on a single theme: "So, does this hurt? Does *this* hurt?" Well, what about *this*?" Eventually he'd gotten her to wince and admit, yes, *that* hurt.

"It's *what*?" she said.

"Tennis elbow." Mickey Duff was a sports therapist with a practice in Illinois; one of four trainers who spent eight or ten weeks on the road with the WPGL tour every year, ministering to players' aches and bruises. He had always struck Lee as a nice young man—maybe five years older than she was—cheerful, helpful, and attentive, but not overly endowed in the brains department. She knew him to say hello to, but this was the first time she had needed his professional attention.

"How can it be tennis elbow?" she cried. "I don't even play tennis."

Mickey weighed this. "Okay," he said reasonably, "we'll call it golf elbow then."

"But—but doesn't it take months, years to develop tennis elbow?"

"Well, now," he said, "tennis elbow's a funny thing."

"Well, what do I do about it?"

"Well, I sure wouldn't play any golf with it for a while."

"Not play any—! Mickey, I'm in the middle of a tournament. I'm *winning*! How can I not play?"

This too was given the consideration it merited. "Yeah," he said, "I can see how that would be a problem."

She waited for some enlightenment, or encouragement,

or anything at all, but nothing came. Mickey just watched her with his friendly, concerned eyes and scratched his soft chin.

They were in the clubhouse massage room, converted for the tournament into an examination room. With her head buzzing with more thoughts and emotions than she could keep track of, she jumped down from the table she'd been sitting on and strode agitatedly down the narrow, carpeted room. At the far end one of the metal lockers was open. She slammed it shut with a vigorous clang that made them both jump, then leaned her forehead against it, trying to sort the clutter in her mind.

Mickey watched her interestedly.

"What if I went ahead and played anyway?" she asked, her head against the cool metal.

"Then it's not going to get any better," he said in his gently admonishing way.

Exasperated, she turned to face him. "Look, Mickey, it isn't that bad now. What I mean is, would it make it more serious? Could I really hurt myself?"

"With tennis elbow? I don't think so, but it might aggravate the symptoms. You might have to lay off for a while. You have to think of your next tournament, Lee."

The hell with her next tournament, she thought, and with the one after that and the one after that. When would she ever be leading the field again, when would she ever have a chance for a major tournament win? Some pros— most pros—played their entire careers without once getting to stand in front of the crowd beside the eighteenth green and accept that wonderful, hokey, oversized winner's check and make a gracious, it-was-a-great-match-and-my-competitors-were-really-tough winner's speech.

For the chance at that, she would gladly risk the next ten tournaments. She turned to face him.

"I'm going to play," she said.

If she was expecting a fight she didn't get one. He had given his advice and if she chose not to take it, she was over twenty-one, and that was all right with Mickey.

But he recommended that she apply an ice pack for twenty minutes every hour that evening and the following morning. And he gave her a Velcro-fastened brace she was to wear around her upper forearm when she was playing.

"Okay," she said, rather than argue, but she knew she wouldn't wear the brace. Anything on her arm would throw her mechanics off. The ice pack, though, that would feel good. She'd put one on as soon as she got back to the motel, showered, and kicked her shoes off in front of the TV set.

For as honest as she was with Peg, she hadn't quite told her the truth about her plans for the evening. She didn't want to go to bed at seven. What she wanted to do was soak for thirty minutes in a hot shower, get into her comfortable, oversized T-shirt, order up a pizza for dinner—pepperoni and green pepper would be heavenly—and sit down with it in front of a good old movie. She'd seen *The African Queen* among the videos in the motel lobby, and that would do just fine. A nice, happy ending.

Not that she hadn't seen it half a dozen times, but that was beside the point. What she really wanted was time by herself, away from everyone, even Peg, so she could hug this fantastic day to herself all over again. And again.

And—no small matter—she wanted to sit down alone with her copy of the WPGL Player Guide to see what the High Desert's purse of $500,000 would mean for a first-place finish, and to dream over it for a while. It was next to impossible that she would actually come away as the winner when all was said and done, of course. One smashing day during which absolutely everything she tried had worked was incredible enough; four in a row would be . . . would be . . . but even a third- or fifth-place finish was bound to bring her more than she had earned all last season. She would pay off the debts that were choking her, she would get her folks' porch refloored, she would live like a human being again, she—

"Lee, for goodness' sake, what are you doing standing around here? Come on, come on, let's get you out of here."

Lee blinked. It took her a few seconds to recognize the horse-faced, big-boned woman in walking shorts and sleeveless tunic as Bonnie Harlow, once a professional golfer herself and now, in her forties, one of the WPGL field directors.

"I—Mickey here was looking at my arm," Lee said. "I thought I might have hurt it."

"Well, I've been looking all over the place for you, lamb," Bonnie told her, laughing. "Let's get over to the press tent."

Bonnie was one of those women who went around calling people "lamb" and "precious," and managed to get away with it by sheer, bubbling force of personality. She had always put Lee in mind of a hardworking Auntie Mame: bright, resourceful, masterful—and underneath it all, more than just a little potty.

"The press tent?" Lee echoed. "Why—"

"Lee, come *on*!" Bonnie urged, tugging at her arm, "I have my cart; I'll drive you over. They just better wait, is all I can say."

Lee shook her head blankly. There were a lot of other things on her mind. The press tent was where the big names went after their rounds to field questions from a respectful audience of reporters on three or four rows of folding chairs. Lee had been inside a press tent only once; to watch the great Kathy Whitworth be interviewed and hope that a little of the magic might rub off. But Kathy Whitworth wasn't playing today.

"Why?" she asked irritably, shaking Bonnie off. "What's the big attraction in the press tent?"

Bonnie looked at her oddly for a moment, then threw back her head and brayed with honest delight.

"*You* are, dummy," she said, and led the way.

It was a few dazed seconds before Lee pulled herself together enough to follow.

Whew. Things were getting heady.

Chapter 5

"I have only one more thing to say on the matter," Vernon Beal said and looked at the others around the table as if expecting to be contradicted. As well he might, Peg thought. Vernon *never* had only one more thing to say, and this hastily called meeting of Cottonwood Creek's five-member board of directors, convened at Vernon's express request, had been no exception. For the last twenty minutes, despite having been repeatedly informed that the board had no say in the decision, he had been asserting the merits of canceling tomorrow's play right then and there, chief among which was prudence.

Vernon could always be counted on for prudence.

His dusty, lawyerly, finicky speechifying had been known to put her to sleep at eleven in the morning. At four in the afternoon, after eighteen holes of golf, he was almost irresistible. Beside her Harry Harrelson had drifted off some time before, breathing quietly, his hands peacefully clasped on his round belly, his round chin sunk on his chest. Harry was a semiretired orthopedic surgeon who claimed to have mastered the art of instant sleep during his days as an intern and often demonstrated it during board meetings.

"There were almost four thousand people here today," Vernon continued. "There will be more tomorrow." He paused, presumably to heighten suspense. "*If* we permit them entrance," he said dramatically, and stopped once more to pull cautiously with his thin lips at the opening in the lid of his plastic coffee cup. It had been cooling for half an hour but Vernon was able to make it look as if it were scalding. "May I submit that, despite Ms. Harlow's lucid explanation of the WPGL's halt-play criteria and procedures—" Here he stiffly inclined his head toward Bonnie"—it is incumbent on us as Cottonwood Creek's governing body to think seriously about the liability consequences for the club should someone be hurt? Furthermore, and this is my final point—"

"Anybody want to know what I think?" Ted Guthrie interrupted, jowls quivering, cheeks mottled with more than their usual purple. Not known for either his patience or his sweet temper at the best of times, the board's president was not bothering to hide his feelings about having been pulled away from the after-play barbecue he had been hosting for his friends (among whom his fellow board members were not numbered). "I'll tell you what I think," he rumbled on, surprising no one. "I think—"

. . . *it's a goddamned load of bullcrap*, Peg silently supplied.

"—it's all stuff and nonsense."

Close enough. Ordinarily Ted went in for earthier language, but apparently he was cleaning up his act in consideration of the presence of a WPGL official in the room. In fairness to Ted, he had been relatively quiet while Vernon had had his long say, emitting little but an occasional stomach rumble or muffled snort of contempt. (It wasn't always easy, Peg had noticed, to say which.)

"In the first place," he went on, speaking directly to Vernon, "you know better than I that there aren't any liability consequences. Acts of God, Vernon. Hell, you're a law-yer. Anyway, what the hell do you think we pay all that insurance for every year?"

As he usually did, Vernon wilted under direct attack by Ted. "Well, yes, that's true enough *theoretically*—"

"In the second place, what kind of probability are we talking about? How many people get killed by lightning in a year? In the United States? Do you know?"

"In the United States?" Vernon repeated uncertainly. "Well, now. As I recall, um, ah—"

Ted peered belligerently around the table. "Anybody happen to know? I mean, since that's what we're talking about, you'd think maybe somebody would try to find out the facts."

Harry, caught on the droop, yanked himself upright. "I believe it's between ninety and a hundred," he said, startling those next to him.

"That's right," Ted said. "Less than a hundred. Out of two hundred and sixty million. That's what, Harry, one out of three million or so?"

But Harry, hands clasped on the convenient protrusion of his belly, was gone again.

"Trust me," Ted went on, "nothing's going to happen tomorrow. We get lightning storms all the time around here, don't we? Has anybody ever got hit playing golf here? Of course not. Look, if a thunderstorm hits, it hits. Like Bonnie says, they tell people over the loudspeakers to clear the course until it's over. What's the big deal? You find the biggest tree around and you get under it and wait it out. I mean, how much brainpower does that take?"

"Obviously, not very much," Frank Ayala said, biting off the words. "Let's all hope it doesn't come up tomorrow, but if it does, let me suggest to the rest of you that the last place you want to be is under the tallest tree around." He eyed Ted with open dislike. "But for you, I'll make an exception. My advice is to head straight for it."

None of them, Peg included, had much liking for the sometimes gross, always arrogant Ted Guthrie, but Harry, Peg, and even Vernon could see his positive side too, albeit grudgingly; his animal-like energy, his stick-to-itiveness, his willingness to take on responsibility and push a job through to completion. Even his dogged, steely chairmanship of a board that disagreed with him at almost every turn.

But the remaining board member, the blue-blooded Frank Ayala—the Ayalas had been one of the seventy-three families that had come to Santa Fe with Don Diego de Vargas in 1693—appreciated none of this. A third-generation state senator and second-generation investment banker, his aversion to Ted was total; an implacable, seemingly constitutional loathing. Peg sometimes thought it was because Frank saw so much of himself in Ted and didn't like what he saw. They were both ambitious, both aggressive, both impatient with others, both endowed with more self-esteem than any one man needed. They even looked alike: burly, thick-necked, square-faced, ruddy. The difference between them lay in bearing. Frank was a thoroughbred and knew it even if he didn't always act it; Ted was the son of an alcoholic greenskeeper at a second-rate golf course and wore his lack of breeding like a badge.

But a thin skin wasn't one of Ted's weaknesses. He grinned at Frank. "Well, that just goes to show. If lightning's so dangerous and I've been doing everything wrong, how come I'm still around? Because when your time comes, it comes. People get hit by lightning sitting in their own house."

"Not if they're careful," Frank said gruffly. "Not if they have a lightning rod."

"Not if they have a lightning rod," Ted said, chuckling from deep in his broad chest, as if Frank had made a joke.

Frank glowered some more.

"May we get back to the point at issue?" Vernon put in, taking heart from what he perceived as Frank's support. "We are not discussing the United States. We are discussing Los Alamos, New Mexico, of which, let me call to your attention, I happen to be a member of the Chamber of Commerce. And let me assure you that one of the distinctions that we do *not* cite in our literature is the well-established fact that New Mexico leads the nation in lightning deaths per capita. I wouldn't care to—"

"Oh, for Christ's sake, Vernon," Ted snapped, "will you lighten up? People are in more danger of getting killed by flying golf balls." He laughed. "Especially if they're standing anywhere near the right-hand sidelines when you're teeing off."

It was high time to intervene, Peg decided. You could argue about lightning storms all you wanted to, but when you started to criticize a man's golf things could get ugly fast.

"Bonnie," she said, do you have anything more to add?"

"Yes, I do," Bonnie said earnestly. Clearly, she had been chafing at the bit. "You have to understand that thunderstorms are a fact of life when you put on golf tournaments. If we canceled a tournament every time there was a possibility of one, we wouldn't have a tour at all. We'd all be home watching bowling on TV."

"The latest forecast shows a seventy percent probability," Vernon pointed out for the umpteenth time.

"Believe me, if there's any danger we'll err on the side of safety," Bonnie told him emphatically. "But if we canceled *now*, it would put *us* at liability in our broadcasting contracts and—my God, it makes me quake in my boots to think about it—all hell would break loose."

36

"You damn well better believe that," Ted said. "From me. I busted my ass getting ASN to put this on."

He had, too. Ted was a major stockholder in ASN—the American Sports Network—and had exerted his formidable powers to get them to include the High Desert Classic among the eight WPGL tournaments that they were contracted to broadcast.

"And if that happened," Bonnie went on, "Cottonwood Creek's chances of getting another WPGL tournament would be about the same as being selected as the site of the next Democratic National Convention. There are simply too many attractive clubs ready to take its place."

Most of them, she didn't have to add, at locations that were a lot easier and cheaper to get to than the highlands of central New Mexico. And all of them in places that were not the lightning capital of the United States.

"And I don't think anybody around this table would like to see that happen," Peg said, hoping they were near to wrapping things up. "We've all worked too hard."

That included Bonnie herself, who had been an effective advocate of putting Cottonwood Creek on the WPGL tour from the start. For her, there was a sentimental attachment. Her father, now dead, had been a well-known golf course architect in the 1950s and 1960s, and Cottonwood Creek had been one of his commissions. Bonnie, then eleven, had been at the opening ceremonies. So had Vernon Beal, somewhat older.

"Well, I think that says it all," Ted said comfortably.

So it did, thought Peg. Vernon had argued his point because he couldn't help quibbling. Frank had challenged Ted because it came naturally. But all of them, every member of the board and a lot of other people as well, had put in an enormous amount of work to get Cottonwood on the professional tour. It was good for their community because it brought in more members. It was good for their souls because it allowed the club to make a handsome contribution to the new Los Alamos public library and the Alzheimer's research project; in all professional golf tournaments—as in no other major sporting events—all income over purses and costs went to charity. And although they didn't like to admit it, it was good for their egos. Having Cottonwood Creek on national television was thrilling. So was hobnobbing with the pros.

"If we're done, I think I'd better go," Bonnie said. "There are about eighty gazillion things I have to do between now and tomorrow morning."

As Vernon began to express a final *pro forma* stipulation to the effect that if anything happened he was taking no responsibility, Ted slapped the table and pushed himself up.

"That's it. Meeting adjourned and I'm outta here."

Chapter 6

"Something's got to be done about Ted," Vernon Beal muttered once the door had closed behind Ted and Bonnie. "That's all there is to it. We need to discuss our options."

"Oh, it's not as bad as all that," Peg said. "He's a little abrupt sometimes, but we can deal with—"

"I'm not referring to his manners, or his ridiculous views on lightning either. I'm referring to his plans for the community in which we live. His unworkable, ill-reasoned, and altogether calamitous plans."

"Ah," Peg sighed. That was what she'd been afraid he was referring to.

"What would you suggest?" asked Harry Harrelson, freshly awake. "Short of murder, of course."

Frank Ayala smiled grimly. "Now hold on, Harry. Let's not set any preconditions."

"You know, you might be right at that," Harry said. He smiled happily, pink and round and cherubic to his toes. "Ah, wouldn't that just solve a lot of problems?"

Vernon gathered his papers together with an irritable flourish. "Come on, fellows, be serious."

Yes, fellows, Peg thought, *be serious*. Or better yet, just don't get started on this subject. Not again.

"Vernon," she said, "it's done, it's all over. The vote's been counted."

"What's done," Vernon said petulantly, "can be undone."

Peg shook her head silently. Not this time, she thought, and not for a long time to come. The Cottonwood Creek Golf and Country Club had just gone through a wrenching four months of rancor and bad blood, and nobody, Vernon excepted, was ready to stir things up again.

"The most explosive issue to hit Los Alamos since 1945," the *Cottonwood Crier* had called it with its usual restraint. But it was true enough that nothing else had split the residents of Cottonwood Creek like this in the thirty-plus years of its existence. Neighbor had fallen out with neighbor in this posh, improbably lush desert community on the Pajarito Plateau just outside Los Alamos; brother had bickered with sister; hitherto rock-solid marriages had shivered and cracked. On Yucca Drive, an incensed eighty-two-year-old man had shot his next-door neighbor's golf cart.

At issue was the conversion of the exclusive residential community to "destination-resort" status. This would include the building of thirty condominiums along the second, fourth, and eighteenth fairways for time-share ownership and vacation rentals, the creation of a nine-hole, three-par course for those unwilling or unable to play eighteen standard holes, and, naturally, the opening of the main Cottonwood course to weekenders, day-trippers from Santa Fe and Albuquerque, and anybody else who felt like playing and had the money to pay the greens fees.

The disadvantages to Cottonwood were serious: there would be crowds and traffic where now there was tranquillity; play would be slow most of the time instead of some of the time; decent starting times would be hard to come by; there would be strangers in the community—loudmouths, bunglers, people with hampers of beer in their carts; who knew what else? And how long would it be before Cottonwood looked like a big-city municipal course, with divots unreplaced, cigar butts on the greens, food wrappers tossed into the rough, and everything in sight taking a beating?

And with it all, many feared, there was sure to be a loss of the cachet that had brought them to Cottonwood Creek in the first place; not so much social cachet, although that was surely part of it, but community cachet, so to speak. Cottonwood had been among *Golf Digest*'s top one hundred golf courses ever since the magazine had begun its annual listing. Would that still be the case when the beautiful, winding, juniper and pinyon forests that bordered the early fairways were replaced with multi-unit condos?

And what kind of serious golf and country club would have a par-three course on its premises? As Frank had angrily put it: "What next, miniature golf with water wheels and steam-puffing dragons?"

When it came to advantages, there was only one, but it was major: money, a lavish infusion that would mean the end of the perpetual, niggling assessments to resurface the tennis courts, recoat the swimming pool, or resod the greens and fairways. And an end to the squabbling and griping that went along with them. More than that, the monthly dues and greens fees of bona fide country club members would be reduced, or even eliminated if things went well enough. And there would be money for better tournament prizes, for better club dances and parties, and for better anything else they thought of.

It wasn't the first time that the idea had arisen, but the Cottonwood Creek board of directors had always nipped it in the bud before.

Before Ted Guthrie, that is.

Theodore Lancelot Guthrie was a relative newcomer to Cottonwood Creek, having bought a lavish house on the

41

twelfth fairway three years earlier. He was boorish, coarse, and loud; his housewarming party had brought the police. But he was also a mover and a shaker. That same year he ran for the presidency of the board and was elected, and things hadn't stopped moving and shaking since. It was Ted who had wheedled or bullied a zoning variance out of the county for the community recreational-parking area after two previous board presidents had given up. It was Ted who had succeeded in getting sewer hookups to the lots in the north quadrant. It was Ted who had gotten the near-defunct greenbelt walking path off the drawing board and into glorious existence.

And it was Ted Guthrie who had begun one board meeting about six months earlier with a simple question: "Hey, listen, have you guys ever thought about turning this place into a resort? I'm talking world-class."

The other four members—Peg, Vernon, Frank, and Harry—had all told him in effect that they had and that it was a lousy idea. Ted, no quitter, raised the subject again in each of the next four meetings with similar results and finally demanded a formal board vote on the proposal. The results surprised no one: four to one against.

Whereupon Ted had called into effect an obscure provision of the bylaws, last used in 1973, under which the president could override his own board and call for a vote of the general membership—that is, the adult residents of Cottonwood Creek—on any proposed capital project involving costs of more than $30,000.

And then he had gone to work with his customary energy. With the help of a small group of like-minded people, he had prepared a comprehensive, four-stage preliminary plan, provided cost estimates, made two-, five-, and ten-year projections, and gotten tentative loan approvals from two banks.

That he was able to do a thorough and impressive job of

it all was no surprise; he was in his element. By profession, Ted was a residential golf course architect, or as he preferred to call himself, a "golf-community revitalizer." Now semiretired at fifty-seven, he had made a substantial living for more than twenty years by modernizing and restoring old-fashioned golf course communities in very much the fashion he was proposing for Cottonwood Creek. His usual fee for analysis, design, and project management was in the $200,000 range.

In this case, he had offered to do it all for nothing; a grateful contribution to the community he now called home. He would even throw in the design of—yes, a miniature golf course ("for the kiddies," Ted said), to be carved out of the barren rough separating the first and eighteenth fairways and requiring no more than a forty-yard relocation of the first tee. No one doubted his ability to do everything and do it effectively. The question was, did they want it done at all?

The bylaws required a simple majority of voters for the project to be approved. The voting had been held two weeks earlier in the community center, with 874 people—96% of the eligible voters—casting ballots. Voting for the project were 439, voting against it were 435. Ted had won with 50.23 percent of the vote.

Most people, whatever their views, had been relieved that it was settled, but Vernon had never stopped fighting, never stopped wanting to discuss their "options." Peg couldn't see it that way. What options? The way she saw it, the vote was in, the decision was made, and they and the rest of the 49.77 percent who didn't like it had better either get used to the idea or look for someplace else to live.

"We could ask for a recall vote." Vernon said. "I've been giving that some thought. "It only takes three-fifths of the board to put it before the membership."

Frank shook his massive head impatiently. "No, you can't recall a formal proposition. Peg's right, it's a *fait accompli*."

"I'm not talking about the proposition now, I'm talking about Ted. Get him out of office once and for all." Modestly, he dropped his gaze. "I, ahum, would be happy to run for the presidency myself."

And there, right there, Peg thought, was the nub of Vernon's boiling resentment. The one significant achievement that had eluded him in this life was the presidency of the Cottonwood Creek Golf and Country Club board of directors. His father had been president from 1968 to 1972, and in this as in everything, Vernon ached to equal his father, a once-celebrated trial lawyer. In pursuit of this goal, Vernon had served on the board for seven two-year terms now, longer than anyone else, and when old Wally McMillan at last announced his retirement as president, Vernon had been a shoo-in, running unopposed—until Ted Guthrie appeared out of the blue to run directly for the presidency without first serving on the board, an unheard-of phenomenon. The vigorous newcomer had won by a landslide. Two years later Vernon had run against him again and once more lost overwhelmingly. It was still inexplicable to Vernon, if not to anyone else, and he had yet to stop simmering over it.

"Vernon," she said gently, "I don't think this is a real good time to split Cottonwood down the middle over a new issue. Let them finish yelling at each other over this one first."

"Besides," Harry said, "doesn't a recall take grounds of malfeasance or moral turpitude?"

"What about all the money he stands to make from developing Cottonwood?" Vernon replied. "Misuse of office."

Harry looked puzzled. "But he's doing it for nothing."

"Oh, please." Vernon snorted. "Can anyone seriously doubt that he's licking his chops at this very moment over kickbacks, and rake-offs, and all manner of under-the-table transactions with his contractor friends?"

"Yes, *I* seriously doubt it," said Peg, who felt it was past time to get off the subject. "There's a lot I don't like about Ted Guthrie, but I don't believe he's doing this to make money. I believe he's doing it for the reasons he says: to contribute something worthwhile to the community—"

Vernon was primly scornful. "Worthwhile!"

"In his view, yes. Did he make money from the walking path? From the sewer hookups? He thinks it'll be good for Cottonwood, whatever the rest of us think."

"And over half of Cottonwood agrees with him," Frank pointed out.

"Barely," muttered Vernon, but with the flagging support of the others it was clear that his heart was no longer in it. "Very well, I don't know what to suggest then."

"I suggest that we put Ted Guthrie on hold and concentrate on the High Desert Classic," Peg said to all of them. "May I respectfully point out that we are in the middle of hosting this highly complex tournament—for the first time? That more than two years of work by two hundred people and twenty committees are coming to a head, and that we are standing here wasting our time bellyaching about Ted when there are a thousand things still to be done? The sponsors are making competing demands, the television people want—"

"Tomorrow," Frank said gruffly. "I've had enough for one day."

The others agreed, and with that the meeting limped to its close.

On the way out, Harry smiled dreamily at Peg as he

slipped on the crumpled fisherman's cap he wore to protect his tender scalp from the high desert sun.

"Do you know, I still rather like the idea of bumping him off," he said wistfully. "Yes, that would certainly get my vote."

Chapter 7

Lou was waiting for her at the entrance to the roped-off driving range, perched on the reinforced bottom end of Lee's golf bag, deeply absorbed in smoking his unfiltered Camel down to the last soggy millimeter. As soon as he saw her he flipped the minuscule stub into the dirt and hopped up, jerking the bag over his shoulder with a grunt.

Simply seeing him did her good: sober, reliable, take-no-nonsense, make-no-nonsense Lou. Lee had awakened that morning with her stomach fluttering. And while that was nothing new in the middle of a tournament, this time it was really something. Nothing as attractive as butterflies either. Bats were more like it.

Then again, when was the last time she had awakened knowing that she was leading a major tournament and on the sports pages of every important newspaper in the country, even if only in the small-print "Results" section?

That was an easy one: Never.

"Is our arm going to hold out?" he asked matter-of-factly, never one to mince words.

"Sure. Touch of tennis elbow is all. No big deal."

She hoped. She had applied the ice pack, she had taken two more aspirin before going to bed, and she had even worn the brace while eating her pizza. And today, except for when she rotated her fist in one particular way, there was no pain, or maybe just the tiniest sense of soreness or perhaps fatigue. As to what an all-out golf swing was going to feel like, that was what she was there for.

"Great," Lou said, his lined face lighting up with the toothy, twisty grin that always came as a surprise to her. "Let's get going, we better loosen up. We're on deck in forty-five minutes."

The "we" and the "our" were happy signs. Lou was anticipating a good day; otherwise it would have been "you" and "your." And, however he did it, his record for predicting Lee's daily performance was better than hers. She noticed too that her bag glistened with fresh leather cream and the clubheads peeping from the top were dazzlingly clean, their faces glowing with a fresh coat of baby oil.

More startling was his hair, slicked down in a style not often seen since the days of Rudolph Valentino, and the electric blue bandanna flamboyantly knotted around his scrawny neck. Lou too was enjoying his increased status.

She hoped she didn't disappoint him. She also hoped he'd knotted the bandanna more loosely than it looked. It was hot and even a little muggy, and she didn't want him dropping with heat prostration halfway through. She also hoped the cauliflowerlike clouds hanging over the mountains to the east weren't going to amount to anything. She didn't want any thunderstorms halting play.

She smiled to herself. Delays were something she usually found herself welcoming. They were the last hope of the also-rans; something—anything—to throw off the momentum of the leaders enough for other people to have a chance at the glory.

But not today, thank you very much.

"I don't want to practice long though," she told Lou. "A small bucket will do."

"Righto, we don't want to overdo," Lou agreed, plopping the bag at her direction into a wire holder at the end of the range, as far as she could get from the TV crew interviewing one of the other players.

But Boyd Marriner, the associate producer from *Golf on Tour*, spotted her as soon as she began her warm-up twists with a couple of clubs across her shoulders and held up his microphone beseechingly. Could she stand being interviewed one more time?

Sure, sure, she mimed nonchalantly, weathered old hand that she was, and stood confidently, her clubs under her arm and a smile on her face as Boyd and the cameraman came to join her. But inside, the bats went at it again.

Actually, her session with the media the day before had been fun. There had been sixteen writers (she knew because she'd counted them) impatiently waiting for her in the press tent when Bonnie delivered her there. And while she had surely bored them stiff with answers they'd heard a million times before ("I was pretty lucky out there. . . . It's going to be really tough from now on, considering the fantastic level of the competition. . . . All I can do tomorrow is play as well as I can and hope for the best."), it had been downright thrilling for her. And everything she'd told them had been the literal truth.

She had especially enjoyed the hour she'd spent outside afterward with Boyd and a cameraman. It had not been a question-answer-question-answer session like the one in the tent. Instead, Boyd had considerately and skillfully drawn her out, telling her what he'd like her to speak about, giving her time to collect her thoughts, and then taping only when she said she was ready.

She had taken to him right away; a low-keyed, older man with a broad, good-natured face, thinning iron-gray hair, and a way about him that made her instantly comfortable. Unlike the other television people she'd run into—hurried and intense, with one eye forever on the clock—Boyd managed to give the impression of having all the time in the world. His quiet sense of humor helped too. So did the obvious fact that he was wholeheartedly rooting for her to win, although of course he couldn't come out and say so.

He had gotten her going by talking about his own time in the Army during the Korean War, and before she knew it she was unselfconsciously chatting away on camera about her military service in Germany and her unlikely start in golf: a two-dollar raffle ticket had won her a weekend, including two introductory golf lessons, at the Army's R-&-R facility in Garmisch. It had been the first time she'd ever picked up a club.

She could tell he was going to make a bigger-than-deserved, up-by-her-own-bootstraps story out of it (her two-year stint in the gorgeous Mosel Valley hardly qualified as a hardship story), and she was probably going to be embarrassed when she eventually saw it. But if he could stand it, she had thought, grinning to herself, she could too. And her parents were going to love it.

This morning he had only a few quick questions to round out yesterday's session, and in ten minutes, with his friendly good-luck wishes still warm in her ears, she was back at work. She began tentatively with the 7-iron and worked her way up through the longer clubs. The results raised her hopes. The twinge was still there, all right, and while swinging the clubs made it more noticeable, it didn't really make it any worse. She had no doubt she could make it through the day and then rest up and go the ice-pack route again before tomorrow's round. How much stress was she going to be putting on her arm, after all? Once you excluded the putts there were no more than thirty-four or thirty-five golf swings in eighteen holes of golf, and even of those, half would be gentle approach shots, not full swings for distance.

Of course she could make it.

For the next half hour she concentrated on blocking the instinctive tendency—the body's automatic means of protecting itself—to alter her swing to favor her left arm. By the time she was done she was sure she'd conquered it. And her arm, thank heaven, didn't feel any the worse for it either, only the littlest bit more sensitive.

"We're gonna have ourselves a hell of a day," Lou said, shouldering the bag once more as they moved toward the starting tee.

"You better believe it," she told him, making herself mean it.

And inside, at least for the time being, the fluttering was down to butterfly intensity.

*　*　*

They were forty-five minutes into the live broadcast when Boyd, back in his chair in the eighteenth-green tower, got one of Mike Bulger's frequent distress calls. This time, however, he had something to be distressed about.

"We just got a warning call from the WPGL people. They're worried about thunderstorms, they're gonna call a halt to play in a couple of minutes. I *knew* we were crazy to shoot a tournament in Arizona, I *knew*—"

"New Mexico, Mike," Boyd said.

"Who cares, what's the difference?" Mike made a sound somewhere between an incredulous laugh and a desperate sob. "How can they be worried about thunderstorms? Where are the clouds? I don't see any clouds, do you see any clouds?"

Boyd scanned the horizon. There were some high, white tufts piled over the Jemez Mountains, but they had hung there all morning without moving. Otherwise the sky was a bright, flat, unthreatening blue. He had to agree with Mike on this one.

"No, I don't see any clouds, but I guess they know something we—"

"Baloney, what could they know? Do you realize we're gonna have over three hours to fill?"

"Mike, it'll probably just be a short break. Thunderstorms move in and out pretty fast. And nobody," he added pointedly, "wants a repeat of 1975."

The 1975 Western Open in Illinois had been the setting for one of the more frightening events in professional golf history. Three topnotch golfers, including Lee Trevino, had been struck by lightning, as had some of the spectators. Amazingly, all had survived. From his bed in the intensive-care ward, Trevino cemented his reputation for gutsy humor when he complained that he had been about to sink an important putt. "Now," he lamented, "they'll probably slap a two-stroke penalty on me for slow play."

Mention of 1975 was usually enough to stop anyone who was griping about safety precautions around a golf course, but not Mike. "Over three hours," he repeated bitterly. "This is gonna be an absolute madhouse." But at last he faced up to the inevitable, winding down with a persecuted sigh. "Well, you better come on over to the trailer when you evacuate the tower. There's a million things to do. And send Skip and What's-her-name over to the clubhouse; we're setting up a studio there. And—"

The discontinue-play siren cut him off, three ear-blasting screeches, *yip-yip-yawp*, repeated over and over. It took no more than a minute or two for Skip and Mary Ann to wrap up their broadcast, but when Boyd followed them down the ladder he was startled by how quickly those benign, pillowlike clouds had moved in. They had scudded in on a wave of humid wind that smelled of earth and rain, rustling branches and leaves as they came. The day was suddenly dark, the air peculiarly charged. The hairs on his arms were standing up.

As he got to the bottom of the ladder the rain began, warm, fat globules that looked like marbles and rattled off hard surfaces like hailstones. Around him, spectators in the grandstands bordering the green pulled jackets or newspapers over their heads and hunkered down to wait it out; they had gotten there hours early to get those seats and they weren't about to give them up without a struggle.

The first stroke of lightning changed their minds; a dazzling burst of white light so intense that tower, green, and grandstand all momentarily disappeared in a bleached, chalky haze. Simultaneously, there was an awful tearing sound, as if the air itself were being ripped apart, and then a terrific, snapping crash, nothing like any thunder Boyd had ever heard. For a second, everyone was frozen—a weird, ashy tableau, as if they were caught in the flash of a colossal strobe light—and then all hell broke loose, with people pouring out of the grandstands, yelling at each other, collaring children, and running for the clubhouse, leaving lunches and umbrellas behind.

Boyd caught a quick glimpse of a shaken Mary Ann and Skip, Mary Ann blinking rapidly and Skip with his mouth hanging open, before the two of them dashed for the clubhouse too. Boyd wasn't long in following. He was shaken as well, and the clubhouse was closer than the trailer.

Inside, Mary Ann and Skip headed for the makeshift studio while Boyd joined the shocked crowd watching from the windows as brilliant, explosive flashes continued to hit all around them. "It's like being at ground zero at White Sands," an awed man near him murmured. But soon the storm moved away from the clubhouse toward the back nine and the lightning began to look more like conventional lightning, the thunder to sound more like conventional thunder, following the flashes by a second, then two, then three. The atmosphere in the clubhouse relaxed perceptibly. There was laughter now, and an air of appreciation rather than fright: "Wow, did you see that one?"

In ten minutes the sky immediately overhead was blue again, the thunder only a distant growl. Boyd jogged across the parking lot to the production trailer. When he climbed the steps and opened the door he got another shock. Entering the trailer was usually like stepping into an earthquake, a bedlam of noise and activity. Most of the eight or ten that were generally crowded into it wore earphones with tiny attached microphones, and everybody was continuously engaged in loud, agitated conversations . . . but not with each other. To an outsider it seemed like chaos; to an insider it wasn't much better.

This time it was different. There was an eerie, intense silence, with most of the technicians crowded around the bank of twenty-six monitors at the front. The same image was on all the screens: Skip Cochrane doing his Dan Rather imitation, looking grave and frazzled at the same time. The technicians were subdued, listening on their headsets. Boyd couldn't hear what was being said.

Only Mike was in his usual state, peppering a nervous assistant director who appeared to be about two weeks out of high school with rapid-fire instructions.

"Mike, what's going on?" he asked when the assistant director returned uncertainly to his stool.

"It's Bob Cooper," Mike said distractedly. "Hit by lightning on the third fairway."

"My God."

Bob was one of their color analysts, a merry kid with red hair, a pug nose, and a Georgia accent, whose golf career had been cut short, as Bob put it, by mediocre play and a set of twins—twins who also had red hair and pug noses and were now a little over two years old.

"How bad?" Boyd asked. He had to clear his throat to get it out.

"Not that bad. He's conscious. They took him to the hospital."

"Thank God for that. Did anyone else get hit?"

"Yeah, a marshal in a golf cart and a couple of idiots who tried to sit it out under an umbrella on the raised tee at sixteen."

"Are they . . . they're not . . ."

"No, no," Mike said impatiently, "nobody's dead. Look, we've got more important things to worry about."

Than life and death? Boyd almost asked, but there wasn't any point. With Mike, nothing was more important than the show he was working on.

"Christ, what a mess," Mike went on. "Play's suspended for an hour, minimum; then they'll see. Well, at least we've got the lightning feature ready to roll, and Nan is editing a highlight package of yesterday's round to throw in if we have to. Vince's over in the clubhouse collaring players and doling them out to Skip and What's-her-name."

"Mary Ann," said Boyd.

"Whatever, whatever. But we *don't* have Ofsted, damn it. She's way the hell out on fourteen, under a tree or something. She's still two strokes in the lead; we *need* her. What if she goes home or something? What if—"

"Mike, calm down, will you? She's probably sitting it out in one of the houses along the fairway. I'll go over to the clubhouse and get the names of the people who live along the fourteenth and call them, okay? When I reach her I'll tell her to get on over here."

"What if you don't find her?"

"Then I'll think of something else. I'll take a golf cart and hunt her down myself." Anything was better than spending the next hour in the truck with Mike. And doing a good turn for Lee appealed to him. She was a nice, wholesome, modest kid, the kind you didn't see much anymore. A little additional exposure might bring her something extra in the way of endorsements.

"Yeah, but what if—"

The telephone behind Mike rang. He tore the receiver off the wall and listened for about five seconds, then started shrieking into it. "Why are you calling the truck *now*? You had all day to figure this out! Hell, I don't know, how should I know? Call Engineering, call—"

Boyd edged out and closed the door quietly behind him.

Chapter 8

"Thank you so much, Mrs. Potter. It's been a real pleasure."

"You're only too welcome, my dear," said the doll-like
figure with the blue-rinsed hair. "Now you just leave the
cart with Juanito down at the clubhouse, and I'll take care
of getting it back."

A wave of her hand and Lee was on her way, driving the
borrowed golf cart over the rise toward the little-used utility
track that Mrs. Potter had assured her was the most direct
route to the clubhouse.

Lee and twenty or so spectators had sat out the storm as
the guests of Mrs. Winfield Potter of 1648 Golden Sunset
Drive, whose house backed up against the right side of the
fourteenth fairway. Lee's professional partners, Ellen Kell,
Susan Torresdahl, and Olga Gronski, had been on the left
side of the fairway when the lightning had struck and had
taken shelter on that side. The elderly Mrs. Potter had been
thrilled to have Lee, fussing over her with iced tea, cookies,
and a discreet offer of her "powder room." Lee, who rarely
passed up a chance like that during a lengthy match, had

gratefully taken her up on it. So had about a dozen others, to Mrs. Potter's obvious dismay.

Lee had appreciated the elderly woman's kindness and had made small talk and even posed for pictures in return, but she had been uneasy and uncommunicative the entire time, worrying about what the delay was going to do to her game.

When the sirens had gone off she had been about to hit a chip shot up to the green, and she had been having another good day. Not as good as the day before, of course (she was likely to go her whole life and never have one like that again), but good enough; she was one under par and still two strokes ahead of Torresdahl and Kell. Olga Gronski was a stroke behind them, and then another three were tied at four strokes back. They were catching up, yes—well why wouldn't they? They were some of the best golfers in the world—but she was still holding them off, holding her own. She hadn't choked under pressure, and that was a tremendous load off her mind. Never before had she been in contention for stakes like these, and she hadn't known what to expect from herself.

Her arm was holding up too. It had gotten a little more tender as the day wore on, but not much worse than the occasional late-game muscle soreness she was used to in arm, or shoulder, or hip, or neck. That was life on the tour. It had never stopped her before.

But she'd never been forced to let her muscles cool down and stiffen up in the middle of play either.

Mrs. Potter had kindly but firmly refused to allow the use of either telephone or television (My word, didn't Lee know that they were dangerous during a lightning storm? No, Lee hadn't known), so she had been unable even to find out how long the delay was going to last, and had sat there on pins and needles until Boyd's call had come—Lee had impulsively grabbed the telephone, hoping for news of the outside world, and it had turned out to be for her.

There would be no play at least until 3 P.M., she was told, but in the meantime she was desperately wanted in the clubhouse. Her groan at a further hour's delay was cut short by Boyd's news of the people who had been hit by lightning.

"Oh, gosh," she'd said with immediate contrition, "and here I am griping about my golf game. I hope they're going to be all right."

But human nature being what it was, it was her golf game she was brooding about again as she steered the electric cart around a curve in the track that took it to the far side of a winding hillock bordering the twelfth fairway. Here, she was on the very perimeter of the course and of the Cottonwood Creek development itself, with nothing but desert stretching off to her right. No wonder the path didn't get much use during a golf game; you couldn't even see the course from there, blocked as it was by the hillock itself and by the rare stand of red maple on its flanks, brick-colored leaves shimmering from the recent downpour.

She was planning her strategy for the seventeenth hole—no carom shots today, if you please—when the winding track straightened out to run alongside a swath that had been cut through the vegetation for a couple of rows of power lines. A few seconds later, she stopped the cart, frowning. She'd seen something from the corner of her eye fifty feet back—seen it, yet not seen it—a shapeless bundle off to the side, a sodden, oversized duffel bag that someone had left while he dashed for cover. Or maybe just a heap of old clothes dumped out in the desert.

Or maybe something else.

Suddenly queasy, she locked the brake, jumped out of the cart, and ran back to see.

Unfortunately, it was something else.

He lay on his back, knees drawn up and thick arms flung out, a beefy older man in Bermuda shorts. Even from ten feet away, she could smell the scorched odor that hung about him. She slowed.

"Are you okay?" she asked thickly, knowing that he wasn't. "Sir?"

She knelt by him and gingerly touched his shoulder, knowing she would jump or even yelp if he suddenly moved or sat up or said anything.

But of course he didn't. He lay inert and heavy, his wet clothes steaming slightly, and that throat-gagging charred smell—like burnt cork—all around. His eyes were closed, his wide face a dull plum color. She couldn't see any injuries, but it was clear that he wasn't breathing. Falling almost instinctively into the pattern that had been drilled into her during her Army training, she pressed two fingertips into the soft part of his neck next to the windpipe. No pulse either.

She lifted her head, yelled "Help!" as loudly as she could, then tilted his forehead back to clear his air passages and got quickly down to work, locking her hands over his sternum and leaning her weight onto him to make rapid, straight-arm chest compressions: *one-and-two-and-three-and* . . .

On the first thrust she felt something give in her left forearm—the arm she'd been babying so jealously all day—and cursed silently, but kept bearing down. By the fourth thrust she knew she was in trouble. A dull, hot ache flowed down her forearm from her inflamed left elbow. Quickly, she shifted position, putting her right hand underneath, which seemed to help a little.

But only a little. The ache was still there, getting sharper by the second. Was this it, then? Was this the way her run for the big time was going to end? Why did *I* have to be the one to find him? she thought bitterly, then felt herself flush at the meanness of the thought.

And yet there it was, mean or not. Willfully, angry at herself, she swept it out of her mind and kept pumping.

. . . *thirteen-and-fourteen-and-fifteen*.

She moved on her knees to his head, cleared his airway again, pinched his nostrils closed, and leaned down. At the touch of the clammy, cool skin around his mouth, the strange, sandpapery feel of his jaw, her resolution faltered. During training they had used plastic protectors for mouth-to-mouth resuscitation, and even that had been a little too intimate for her. Now her stomach heaved at—

More unworthy thoughts. She shook her head, bent and blew two quick breaths into him, seeing his chest fill like a balloon, then deflate again. Still no pulse, no breathing on his own.

She positioned herself over his chest, noticing for the first time that there was an injury visible after all. His outflung left hand had been terribly burned, a deep, gray-white—

She looked sharply away and forced herself back to chest compressions.

"What . . . I . . . What's happened here?"

An elderly man with a furled golf umbrella under his arm was standing apprehensively a few feet up the track. "Is he—"

"Go get help," Lee told him tersely. "There's a medic station at the clubhouse. Take my cart, it's right over there."

The man goggled at her, then appeared to collect his wits. "Yes. Of course. Immediately."

Lee was back to chest compressions before he'd taken two steps. An exhausting, seemingly endless five minutes later, the medics pulled up in their truck. Her arm was throbbing now. She hadn't bothered to favor it at all, probably as a sort of unconscious penance for the selfish, small-minded resentment she'd felt a few minutes before.

"Pulse? Breathing?" asked the younger of the two men, a skinny kid with two earrings in his right ear.

"No, nothing," she said, and bent to the task again.

"Get back for a minute," he told her. With his partner, a black-bearded Latino, he set a container on the ground and opened it; something like an oversized fishing-tackle box with a monitor in the flip-up top. Grateful to be relieved, Lee sank back while they pulled up the knit shirt of the figure on the ground, greased a few areas of its torso, and applied two electrical leads to its chest and one to its side.

Both men stared intently at the screen in the box. Moving as if her legs were cast from lead, Lee went to look too.

The men glanced at each other. "Asystole," the bearded one said.

She didn't have to ask what it meant. That was all too clear from the flat, motionless line on the screen. She'd seen it in a hundred disease-of-the-week TV specials.

"Damn," she murmured.

"Thanks a lot for trying, ma'am," the bearded one said politely. "You did your best."

Lee shrugged uneasily. He had made her feel guilty. Had she meant, "Damn, I'm sorry he's dead?" or had she meant, "Damn, I'm sorry I bunged up my arm and blew my chances for no good reason"? She wasn't sure herself.

The kid with the earrings removed the leads. "It's kind of funny," he mused, "I just saw him an hour ago, all full of pep, and now . . . jeez."

"Then you know who it is?" Lee asked.

"Sure," he said, as if astonished that Lee didn't. "This here is Ted Guthrie."

"Who?" said Lee.

Chapter 9

"Ted Guthrie . . ." said Peg, blowing out her cheeks. "I still can't believe it. It's positively weird."

"Why is it weird?" Lee asked abstractedly, going through her warm-up routine again, twisting and stretching with two clubs across her shoulders as they waited near the fourteenth tee for the "resume play" signal, due to go off at 3:50 according to the announcement fifteen minutes earlier.

The passage of an hour's time at the clubhouse in Peg's hearty, down-to-earth company (Boyd had understandingly accepted her reluctance to be interviewed after all) and the consumption of an iced coffee, a box of chocolate-covered raisins, and two more aspirin had dulled the horror of the scene on the path, revived her spirits, and brought her natural optimism back. Not all the way back, but far enough to make her think that she was capable of finishing the round after all if she took no chances. The sharp pain in her arm had diminished to a tender, throbbing ache that she thought she could handle for what was left of the round. All she had to do was get through five more holes—one at a time, as Lou said—and then she'd be able to rest up until tomorrow.

She would apply the ice pack religiously, all through the night if necessary. She would wear the brace while she was sleeping. She would see Peg's orthopedic surgeon, she would think good thoughts, she would write home more often. Just five more holes was all she needed. Even Peg, nothing if not hardheaded, was upbeat about her chances.

But then she hadn't told Peg she'd rehurt herself pushing on Ted Guthrie's sternum.

"I already told you why it's weird," her friend said. "Here we've got three or four thousand people on the course, maybe more. Bing, we get a lightning storm. People get hit all over the place. And who's the only one who dies? Theodore Lancelot Guthrie, the most roundly hated man for miles, the very man who 49.77 percent of the community would give their eye teeth to get rid of."

A spark of grim humor flickered across Peg's face. "Maybe not quite so sensationally, however."

"So what are you saying," Lee asked, "that it wasn't an accident?"

Peg shrugged. "Well, yes, I guess that's what I'm saying."

Lee finished stretching and slipped the clubs into her bag. "That it was what? Foul play? Murder?"

Peg wasn't ready to put it quite as baldly as that. "I just can't help wondering if it was really accidental, that's all. It's too . . . bizarre. I mean, the one guy who—"

"Peg, how could you possibly arrange to murder someone with a lightning bolt?"

"Well, I know—"

"Unless you have some pretty big-time connections, I mean."

Peg's wonderful foghorn laugh must have carried to the eighteenth green, and a moment later Lee was laughing with her, a welcome, irresistible laugh straight from the belly, the first time her stomach muscles had unknotted since the moment she'd seen that crumpled duffel bag that hadn't been a duffel bag.

They didn't stay unknotted for long. While they were still laughing, a melancholy wail from the loudspeakers signaled that play was resuming. A marshal nodded Lee toward the tee box, the field interviewer and his cameraman moved in a little closer, and the patiently waiting crowd around the tee stirred and murmured, as they were undoubtedly stirring and murmuring at each of the other seventeen tees.

It was time to see what she had left. Peg smiled her most encouraging smile, gave Lee a quick thumbs-up, and withdrew behind the rope to join the gallery. An edgy, taciturn Lou held out the driver for her. She hadn't told him she'd reinjured herself either, but Lou didn't always have to be told things to know them. When she strode to the box, the gallery responded with a warm patter of applause, as they'd been doing all day long; not Arnold Palmer applause or Betsy King applause by a long shot, but it was more than she was used to and she responded with a grateful dip of her head.

But she was scared. She'd done her warm-up exercises but hadn't taken any practice swings; she'd been afraid to. Well, re-teeing from the fourteenth was a good way to start. It called for a fairly short drive of about 200 yards to just short of a dry streambed, then another 140 yards to the hole. Easy shots. Yesterday she had confidently—and successfully—chosen a more muscular approach, clearing the streambed on her drive and then having an easy 110-yard lob to the green. She'd birdied with ease, but that was yesterday.

She took her stance and focused her concentration. The crowd quieted. She was halfway through her takeaway when the hot twinge in her arm told her that it wasn't going to work, that it was over, and the muddled, spastic downswing confirmed it for everyone to see. She shanked it, like the rawest hacker. The ball skidded crookedly off to the side and into the junipers on the right, 60 yards from the tee.

She let the club fall to the grass and clutched her burning forearm, her eyes closed, sick and dizzy with disappointment. She'd really thought . . . she'd really hoped . . . All that work, all those months of living a tramp's life, this week to Tennessee, next week to Delaware, the one after that to Pennsylvania; traveling by bus, by the "rabbits' car pool," by plane when she had to because time was short; all those life-or-death Monday qualifying rounds that the nonexempt players had to go through, all those fifty-nine-cent hamburgers, all the heartsore nights in dreary motel rooms when she'd failed to make the cut, all the evenings in grubby laundromats . . .

The previous evening she'd gone ahead and looked up the standard breakdown for a tournament with a $500,000 purse. The winner here was going to come away on Sunday with $75,000. Third place brought $34,000. Even a tenth-place finish would have meant almost $11,000. She could have covered her costs for almost a year, she could have—

Lou was standing in front of her, his seamed, sun-weathered face pinched with concern.

"Arm?"

She nodded, blinking to keep the tears back. "I'm out," she murmured.

For a moment he seemed to sag, then shook it off. "Hey, don't take it so hard, there'll be plenty of other tournaments. You got all the time in the world to get there."

She nodded again, suddenly unable to speak. Sure, she had lots of time to get there, wherever "there" was, but how much time did Lou have? How many more years could he lug those gigantic bags around? How many of today's pros would want him to? What would a win like this have meant to him? Lee had figured out his 6 percent of her earnings too: $4,500 if she'd won, and of course in that case she would happily have followed tradition and made it 10 percent: $7,500. When was the last time he'd seen money like that? What chance did he have to ever see it again?

"Lou, I'm so sorry . . ."

"No big deal," he said gruffly. "Win some, lose some."

Then, to her amazement he took an awkward step forward and put his arms gingerly around her, the first time in her memory he had touched her or anyone else other than for a handshake. It took a moment for her to realize that he was trying to shield her, to give her another few seconds' protection from the television cameraman who was zooming in on her disappointment-streaked face. The only problem was that the top of Lou's slicked-back hair barely made it to her chin.

And suddenly she was smiling. It was on the shaky side, but it was a smile.

"Lou," she said, gesturing at the cameraman and the interviewer, who were now closing in on her, intent on a public postmortem, "will you talk to them for a minute? I have to tell the marshal I'm picking up."

"*Me?*" he croaked, stunned. He swallowed and turned obediently toward the advancing camera crew.

It was above and beyond the call of duty, and she would apologize to him later, but she needed a few seconds to herself. She walked to the edge of the green to inform the marshal that she couldn't continue, then stood alone, her head bent, taking three or four deep breaths. The gallery, like most golf galleries, was sensitive to players' occasional needs for privacy. They watched, but they didn't intrude. Even Peg held back.

When she went back to Lou and the camera crew, she

found her caddie in surprisingly high gear, staring head-on into the camera as he explained her situation to the world.

"It's from when she was giving artificial respiration to the dead guy," he was loudly declaiming in his ever-tactful manner.

Laughter bubbled inappropriately in her throat, but she fought it primly down. What a one-of-a-kind he was.

When the interviewer saw her, he cut Lou off with a quick thank-you and shifted his attention to her. The cameraman swung around.

Lee squared her shoulders, put her smile more firmly in place, and prepared to play the gracious sports star.

One last time.

Chapter 10

"Detective Torres," Ruben said automatically into the telephone, glancing at his watch at the same time. It was 4:50 P.M., almost time to leave for the day. For the last few minutes his mind had been drifting to his daughter's fourth birthday party at the McDonald's on Trinity Drive at 6:30, complete with an appearance by Ronald McDonald. Ruben had promised to be there to introduce Ronald to the kids, and now he was thinking that if he left a little early he could swing home first for a leisurely shower and a change of clothes—

"Hello, Ruben," a lively voice shouted in his ear, "this is Dr. Minkoff. I'm at the Medical Center."

"Hello, Doc, they got you working on Guthrie?"

"Yes, indeed they do, and I have a few interesting things to show you."

Ruben glanced at his watch again. Dr. Nathan Minkoff was a deputy medical investigator, but unlike his fellow investigators in New Mexico's OMI—Office of the Medical Investigator, headquartered in Albuquerque—he was a full-fledged physician too, and not only that but a certified and experienced forensic pathologist. Dr. Minkoff had put in two grueling decades in the big time—the New York City Medical Examiner's Office—loving every minute of it to hear him tell it, and then, newly widowed at sixty-three, he had called it quits and moved to Los Alamos to be near his married daughter. He had pulled a few strings with his New Mexico counterparts and gotten himself appointed as a part-time "uncompensated consulting deputy MI," the only one there was or ever had been.

Dr. Minkoff was a man who loved his field. ("We medical examiner types are the only ones who get to autopsy nice, healthy bodies," he had once told Ruben. "Regular doctors only see *sick* corpses.") He was a nice, talky old guy too; Ruben had already learned a lot from him. But "a few interesting things" usually meant a good hour's worth, and Ruben had Ronald McDonald to think about.

"I tell you, Doc," he said, already on his feet, closing drawers and putting away files, "Sam Lewis is the officer who went out to the scene, so I guess you could say this is his case. Let me switch you."

But Dr. Minkoff was too quick for him. "No, no, no," he shouted before Ruben could hit the button. "I just talked to Sam. But, Ruben, I think maybe this ought to be *your* case."

The detective ran a hand through his dark, prematurely thinning hair and sat slowly down again. "*My* case? You're not telling me we've got a homicide? Wasn't the guy hit by lightning?"

"He was, yes. Well, indirectly."

"Indirectly? How does a person—"

"Look, Ruben, I'm not sure what we have here, but I think you ought to come over and take a look. I think we're going to have to rule out suspicion of homicide."

That put a different cast on things. "Rule out suspicion

of homicide" was forensic jargon. When you sent a sample of something to the crime lab with that instruction, it meant that you were suspicious, that you were asking the lab to consider the possibility of homicide, to make the appropriate tests, to formally rule it out—or in.

Ruben sighed and reached a lanky arm to the top of the bookcase behind him for his old green Oakland A's cap. "I'll be right over."

Ronald McDonald was going to have to fend for himself.

* * *

Minkoff was waiting for him in the gleaming, white-tiled room in the basement of the rambling Los Alamos Medical Center on West Road, standing at a waist-high metal table, one of two, on which lay Guthrie's body, naked to the waist, discreetly sheet-covered below. It had only been a few hours since the president of the Cottonwood Creek board of directors had died, and the body was still fresh; no nasty smells, no discoloration to speak of, and no Frankenstein-like, sutured-up autopsy incisions. Indeed, autopsies were rarely done here. When called for they were performed at OMI's central laboratory at the University of New Mexico in Albuquerque.

The doctor greeted him cheerfully, a molelike little man with a small, round head, tiny, myopic eyes peering earnestly through thick trifocals, and a receding, barely perceptible chin. He was wearing his usual blue work smock. For reasons of his own, he eschewed the standard white laboratory coat.

"Hello, Doc, what have you got?"

"That's the question, all right," Minkoff said. "Tell me, what was this man doing out there in the middle of a lightning storm, do you know?"

"Sure, he was on the committee that's running the tournament and he was one of those guys who likes to keep his finger on things. He was just cruising the golf course, looking for problems before they happened."

"Cruising? On foot?"

"I guess so. Why not?"

"In the middle of all that lightning?"

"No mystery there, Doc. Lightning didn't bother him."

"Come again?"

"He wasn't scared of it. He was laughing at the rest of the committee about it just last night." He looked down at Guthrie's gray, fleshy body. "He's sure not laughing now."

"Listen, are you positive nobody was with him when he died? He was alone?"

Ruben was becoming impatient. "Look, Doc, if somebody was with him, I haven't heard about it. Now how about just telling me what you have?"

Minkoff nodded crisply. "Very well. You see the burns for yourself." He gestured at Guthrie's left hand.

Ruben leaned over it. The palm looked as if it had been deeply seared with a red-hot iron rod. Minkoff turned the hand over, pushing against the still-developing rigor mortis. The first two knuckles were burned as well.

"Okay, I see," Ruben said.

"These would seem to be the entrance burns," Minkoff told him. "There are exit burns, much less severe, on his buttocks, shoulders, and heels. Help me turn him over and I'll show you."

"I'll take your word for it, Doc."

Minkoff shrugged. "Fine. Now then, that's it; there are no other injuries that I could find, although you understand I'm somewhat limited here."

Ruben nodded, waiting.

"Let me come straight to the point, Ruben. These are not the typical sequelae of a direct lightning strike. Where were the scorched clothes, the melted pen in the pocket? And where is the pathognomonic arborescent erythema we have every right to expect? Tell me that."

"Doc, I can't even tell you what they are, let alone where they are."

"For another thing," Minkoff went on, "the burns on his hand are not what we would expect either. How does a person manage to be struck by lightning on the palm of his hand? Tell me that if you can."

"Maybe he was holding his hand up to protect himself against the rain?"

Minkoff dismissed this with a snort. "With his palm uppermost?" He demonstrated, cringing against an imaginary storm. "Unlikely. Besides the burns are far too deep. Lightning produces charring of the skin, singeing of the hair, yes; but not this deep, rutted lesion. The duration of a strike is less than one ten-thousandth of a second, much too short to produce third-degree burns."

"What then?" Ruben asked.

"Guess," Minkoff said happily.

"Doc, I really—well, would he have been holding something in his hand that attracted the lightning?"

"Now you're talking," Minkoff said.

"An umbrella, maybe? A golf club? And the metal conducted the electricity and that's what made the burn marks?"

"You took the words right out of my mouth," Minkoff said. His points made, he pulled the sheet up over Guthrie's face and arranged it with surprising tenderness.

Ruben leaned thoughtfully against the table behind him. "All right, then, what's the problem? What's suspicious?"

"You read Sam's report?"

"Yes. Well, not all that carefully," he admitted, "but there wasn't that much to read."

"I read it too. Carefully." He looked meaningfully at Ruben through his bottle-bottom lenses.

"And?"

"And this mysterious umbrella, this golf club—where is it mentioned in the report?"

Ruben's brow creased. "Maybe he didn't do a thorough search, Doc. It wasn't a crime scene, after all, just—"

Minkoff was shaking his head. "I already talked to him. He says there wasn't anything in the immediate area. And Sam's one of the observant ones."

Ruben nodded his agreement. He was starting to feel that Minkoff had a point. "All the same, I think maybe I'll send him out again for a better look."

"I think that's a good idea."

"Maybe Guthrie convulsed, flung whatever it was into the bushes."

"Maybe," said Minkoff, patently unconvinced. "And somebody ought to talk to the one that found him, that lady golfer."

Ruben's nod of agreement was a shade dejected this time. The Los Alamos Police Department was a small outfit. If Sam went out to comb the site again, "somebody" was going to be him, Ruben. And the sooner the better. Now, to be exact. Witnesses at traumatic events had a way of getting mixed up about what they'd seen or hadn't seen, even after a few hours. That meant he was going to be late for Elena's party. He'd have to call Rosie and explain before he went out to find the golfer. But with a little luck he might still make it before it was over.

"There's something else," Minkoff said. "The exit burns. Superficial, not much to look at, but doesn't the placement make you wonder? Shoulder, buttocks, heels?"

Ruben's knowledge of electrical forces wasn't everything it might have been. "I don't understand."

"Electrical current," Minkoff said, his face brightening at the chance for a mini-seminar, "passes through the body in the shortest possible path from the *conductor*—the electrocuting object—to the exit site or sites, the place or places where the person is touching the ground or a grounded object. In a standing person, the burns would be on the soles of the feet, do you see? But in this case, buttocks, shoulders, and heels would all appear to have been in contact with the ground or a grounded object. There may have been other parts as well—there is not necessarily a burn at every exit site—but these parts at least." He waited for Ruben to draw a conclusion.

"Buttocks, shoulders, heels . . ." Ruben reflected. "He could have been *sitting* when he was hit—in a golf cart, for instance. And if he was, what happened to the cart?"

Minkoff was nodding rhythmically while Ruben spoke. "Sitting . . ." Minkoff said, ". . . or lying on his back, the way he was found."

Ruben frowned, genuinely caught up at last. "On his back?"

"And what," Minkoff added softly, "would anyone be doing lying on his back in the middle of a thunderstorm?"

Chapter 11

"Mmmm," Dr. Harrelson said, his genial features puckered into a pensive scowl. Delicately, he rotated Lee's forearm one more time. "Well, now. Mmmm." He shook his head slowly back and forth and clucked sympathetically.

Oh my gosh, Lee thought nervously, what have I gone and done to my arm? Is that it for golf? Am I through at twenty-three? What else do I know how to do? Would they take me back in the Army?

"Now, we can't know for certain until we see some X rays," he said, giving her arm back to her, "but I think I can give you a fairly confident preliminary diagnosis. The lay of the land, so to speak."

Lee had tracked the orthopedic surgeon down at a terrace table, where he had been enjoying a well-deserved Löwenbräu after responding handsomely to the paramedics' call for help with the lightning injuries. But he had good-naturedly left his beer, jammed his crumpled canvas hat over his gleaming head, and suggested using Mickey's space in the clubhouse massage room for a preliminary examination of Lee's arm. He had taken a long, thorough look at it, his stubby fingers playing over her arm with amazing gentleness.

She steeled herself for his verdict. "Yes?"

"It seems to be acute lateral epicondylitis," he told her gravely.

Her mouth went dry. "Acute . . . What does that mean?"

"It's an inflammation," Dr. Harrelson said, "or perhaps a small tear, of the common tendon connecting the extensor muscles to the lateral epicondyle." He tapped her elbow. "Considering what you've told me, I should say it was caused by overtaxing of the extensor carpi radialis group as well as the extensor carpi ulnaris." He paused to give it further thought. "On the other hand," he said, speaking mostly to himself, "it could involve the abductor function of the extensor pollicis—"

"*Dr. Harrelson*," Lee blurted, "please! Can't you just tell me in English?"

"In English?" He looked surprised. "Yes, well, in English I suppose you'd say you have a moderately severe case of tennis elbow."

"Tennis . . ." Limp with relief, she fell back against her chair, laughing.

"Well, I don't know that it's anything to laugh about, young lady," Dr. Harrelson told her severely. "You continue putting this kind of stress on your elbow and you're going to end up with a full-blown case of traumatic arthritis, which is no joking matter. Let me assure you, I've had to operate on more than one elbow no older than yours. And it wasn't very pretty in there, I can tell you."

Lee winced. "I'll be careful," she said, properly chastened.

Dr. Harrelson accepted this with his ready smile. "Now, I want you to stop in at the medical center for an X ray in case there are any other problems, which I doubt, but we don't want to take any chances. Can you tolerate aspirin? Good, that will relieve the inflammation. Other than that, ice is the ticket until the swelling subsides. Heat later. For now, ice, rest, and aspirin will do the trick until you see your own physician at home."

"Home is Portland, Oregon, I'm afraid."

"Well, that might be the best place for you for the next four to six weeks."

She blanched. "Four to six *weeks?*" That meant no Denver Open, no Omaha Classic, no—

"If you value the rest of your career, yes," he said flatly. "No reason to look so glum about it either. At your age it'll pass in the blink of an eye."

Sincerely wishing she could blink the next six weeks away—it would do her bank account less damage—Lee gratefully thanked him for his help.

"My pleasure, I assure you." He beamed at her. "Even though you've made my paramount ambition that much harder. *I* was planning to set a new course record here, you know. All I had to do was shave a mere thirteen strokes off my best score."

Lee smiled back at him. "Well, now it's only sixteen."

"Child's play," Dr. Harrelson agreed. "But it's a moot point anyway. The course layout and scoring are going to be quite different by the time Ted Guthrie and his—" He stopped. "Odd how I can't seem to make myself remember he's dead. You'd think a doctor wouldn't have that problem." He reached impulsively for her hand—her good hand—with both of his. "That was a wonderfully unselfish thing you did out there, Lee. I'm sorry it had to put you out of work. I was pulling for you, you know."

"That's the way the breaks fall," Lee said, getting down from the examination table. "I've had plenty of good ones, so I guess I can stand a few bad ones." Funny, here she was cheering *him* up, but he looked so genuinely woeful on her behalf. "Well, I think I'll pack it in here," she said. "It's been a heck of a day. I'll stop on the way back and get that X ray."

"Ice, aspirin, rest," were his parting words.

Before going to the locker room to get her things she wanted to find Lou and pay him what she owed him. In addition to their percentage of winnings, tour caddies were paid anywhere from $300 to $500 a week. In Lee's case it was $300, all of which she wished she could give him— this string of calamities certainly wasn't his fault—but it was simply impossible. For someone like her, someone just managing to survive on the tour, finishing a competition out of the money was a catastrophe: travel costs, room costs, food costs, caddie wages—all of it expended for nothing. Her checking account was in disastrous shape, and now there was no hope of replenishing it for four to six weeks. Lou would have to accept $200. It was a long way from the $7,500 he might have ended up with, and Lou had expenses too, but it was all she could manage, even if she headed straight back to Portland tomorrow, which was exactly what she intended to do. Feeling thoroughly sorry for herself.

With the clubhouse off-limits to caddies, she was fairly sure she would find him in the caddie yard, the roped-off area near the bag room. Facing him wasn't going to be any fun. Sure, he'd only worked about half the week, so $200 was fair, but now he was out of a job until the next tournament, assuming he could find one then. Not that he was the kind to raise a fuss. Lou kept his worries to himself.

But when she saw him standing with Boyd Marriner and Bonnie Harlow, she veered off. In the last hour she'd had all the sympathy she could stand. She turned back the way she'd come but it was too late.

"What a miserable break, Lee!" Bonnie called, catching sight of her. "You poor thing, I'm so sorry."

"Lee!" Boyd said simultaneously, saving Lee a reply.

"We've been trying to track you down. I'm hoping I can talk you into doing me a big favor."

"A favor?" she said confusedly.

"You know, one of our color analysts, Bob Cooper, was hurt out there today. He's going to be out for a month or so, and I was hoping to tempt you into subbing for him until you're ready to play again. Four hundred bucks a day and expenses, and it won't put any strain on your arm. What do you think?"

She stared at him, not sure if she could believe what she'd just heard. What did she think? She thought she was ready to kiss him for an offer like that. Whether it was really a favor to him or something he'd generously set up to help her get through a difficult patch she didn't know—possibly some of each, but either way the dark clouds over her head had suddenly parted.

"Who knows?" he added, smiling. "You might even like television work. Amazing as it sounds, I hear some people do."

"I'd love it!" she answered before he had a chance to change his mind. "Thank you, it would be wonderful." If you asked her, *Golf on Tour* already seemed overendowed with color analysts, but who was she to argue?

"It'll give you something to tide you over," Bonnie said, looking genuinely pleased for Lee. "Believe me, I know how tough it is to make ends meet when you're just starting out."

Not from experience, she didn't. Cottonwood Creek had been just one of many lucrative country club commissions that had come the way of her famous golf-course-architect father, and he had seen to it that her early golfing days had been amply financed; a far cry from Lee's scrambling struggle to survive. Still, it had been kindly meant and Lee was grateful.

"Well, I gotta be going," Lou said abruptly and turned away.

"Lou, wait," Lee said. "I was looking for you. I just wanted to let you know I'll be . . . I'll be paying you for the entire week, and I'm just sorry it didn't work out any—"

"I don't take money for nothing," Lou said bluntly. "I only worked three and a half days."

She could have kicked herself for embarrassing him in front of strangers. "But I only meant—"

"Lou, listen," Boyd interjected. "I could use another runner too. It's a hundred and twenty-five a day plus meals. What do you say?"

Lou gave him a long, doubtful look. Was the guy a one-man employment office? "I don't run," he said with dignity.

"He doesn't mean *run* run, darling," Bonnie said, trying to be helpful but receiving only a scowl in return. Trilling "darling" at him was not the way to Lou's heart.

"What do they do, then?" he asked grumpily.

"All kinds of things. Get things, do errands—" She turned to Boyd for help. "This is *your* job. Why am *I* explaining it?"

"Actually," Boyd said to Lou, "they do whatever comes up. They go find people, they move equipment, they carry stuff, they go to the hardware store—"

"For what?" Lou interrupted, not an easy man to talk into $125 a day.

Boyd laughed. "Are you kidding? On-location TV is the best thing that ever happened to the hardware business. Last night I had to go to True Value for two wing nuts and a circuit tester. Everybody does it. Bonnie was there too, getting this whole—"

Bonnie winced. "Never reveal a lady's secrets, pet. Let's just say it was a rather complete laundry list, from alligator clips to curling irons, and leave it mercifully at that."

Lou weighed their comments. "So what a runner is, is a gofer," he concluded.

Boyd smiled. "You got it."

"I'll take it," Lou said.

"Great, glad to have you," said Boyd. "Glad to have you both. Why don't you show up at the truck at seven-thirty tomorrow morning—"

"Good grief," Bonnie exclaimed. "I was supposed to be meeting with the course marshal five minutes ago." She was pulling out her cellular telephone when it rang. "I know, love, I'm on my way," she said into it before giving the caller a chance to speak. "I'll be—" She stopped short. "Yes, this is she," she said solemnly. "Yes, I do. In fact I'm speaking with her right this minute. Yes, of course. We're in the caddie yard. You'll find it near . . . Yes, we will, er, shall. 'Bye."

"It's a police detective named Torres," she told Lee. "He wants to talk to you."

"To me? About what?"

Bonnie shrugged. "He didn't say."

"Well, you're about to find out," Lou said, gesturing with his chin toward someone just entering the yard. "That's him. The guy's got 'cop' written all over him."

Not to Lee, he didn't. A slender man in his thirties, beak-nosed and gangling, dressed in T-shirt and jeans, and with a scuffed, old Oakland A's cap on his head, he looked more like one of the grounds crew than like a detective.

But of course Lou was right. The man approached them with his wallet held out to show his badge. "Detective Torres, Los Alamos PD," he said. Then to Bonnie: "Miss Ofsted?"

"Don't I wish," Bonnie said, gesturing at Lee.

"Miss Ofsted, I understand you're the one who found Mr. Guthrie."

"Yes."

"I'd appreciate it if you could answer a few questions for me."

"Questions?" Lee said. "About—?"

"Why don't we go someplace . . ."

"We were just leaving," Boyd said quickly. See you in the morning, Lee."

"Ohmigod," Bonnie said, "the course marshal! G'bye all!"

"I guess I'll go get your stuff cleaned out," Lou said to Lee, a little more reluctantly than the others—nosiness was one of his vices—but in a moment he too was gone.

"I guess maybe here is good enough," Torres said, smiling. There were only five or six other people in the yard; most of the foursomes hadn't come in yet. Every now and then Lee could hear applause from the eighteenth green. She tried not to listen.

"Miss Ofsted, when you found the body you were alone, is that correct?"

"Yes, I was heading back to the clubhouse."

"Was there anybody else around?"

"No, I don't think so."

"Do you remember seeing any objects near it?"

"Objects?" Lee echoed.

"Yes, anything at all."

"No, nothing. Of course, even if there was I probably wouldn't have noticed." She shivered.

"Nothing made of metal?"

"Metal? Why would you—no, I don't remember anything."

"Nothing he might have been holding in his hand? Golf club? Umbrella?"

She shook her head. "You think someone killed him, don't you?" she asked, startling herself. Peg's ruminations had made more of an impression than she'd realized.

If Torres was surprised he didn't show it. "It's hot in the sun. You want something to drink?"

"A Coke would be nice." She led him to the little snack bar near the locker rooms, deserted at this point in the round.

A big-screen television set reported tournament progress to the empty room. ". . . which puts Torresdahl firmly in the lead," Skip Cochrane was yapping. "What an incredible putt, Mary Ann! A thirty-foot, uphill—"

"Big deal," Lee muttered uncharitably to herself and turned the TV off while Torres went to the soft drink machine.

He came back with her Coke and a root beer for himself. When he sat down he took off his cap and put it on a chair. He was nearly bald, with a few strands of black hair running backward over the crown of his head. "Now what would make you say a thing like that?" he asked conversationally, popping the can's top. "That I think someone killed him."

"For one thing, you're here asking me questions about it. I don't think a detective would be involved in investigating a simple accident."

He said nothing.

"Well, would you?"

"Probably not," he said, smiling again. He seemed like a nice guy. She realized suddenly that he reminded her of Graham, not in his looks but in his bearing: straightforward, self-contained, quietly authoritative, with something steely just under the surface. Possibly it was a manner detectives developed. Probably worked pretty well with crooks. It had worked pretty well with her too, as far as Graham was concerned. Why, she wondered a little irritably, was she thinking so much about Graham lately? They had agreed— she had insisted—

"What else?" Torres said.

Lee blinked. "What?"

"What else makes you think I might think he was murdered?"

"Oh. I understand everybody hated him, but I guess you already know that."

His expression made it clear that he hadn't. He set the root beer on the table. "Run that by me again?"

"Well, I didn't mean *everybody*, of course, but a lot of people."

Briefly, she told him what she remembered of Peg's remarks, which wasn't much. He took down Peg's name and phone number in case he couldn't find her in the clubhouse and looked at his watch. "Thanks for your help, Miss Ofsted—"

"Wait a minute," she said abruptly. "There was a man. I just remembered. *He* had an umbrella."

Already partway out of his seat, Torres slid back into it. "Near Guthrie?"

"No, not when I got there, but then I yelled for help and a minute later—well, I don't know how long; maybe it was even less—he was there."

The table, one leg shorter than the others, tilted as Torres leaned forward on it. "But you're sure he came in response to your call? He couldn't have been there before?"

No, Lee said slowly, she wasn't sure. She hadn't seen him coming; suddenly, he was just there. He *might* have been hidden among the maple trees or behind one of the small hills. It was possible he'd heard her coming and hidden.

"What did he say?"

She tried to think. "I don't remember. 'What's going on?' or something like that. He seemed pretty shocked." She smiled weakly. "Not that I'm anybody to talk. Anyway, I asked him to get help and a little while later the medics showed up."

Torres was jotting notes in a pocket-sized pad. "What'd he look like?"

She frowned. "I don't know . . . gray-haired, not too tall . . . not too fat . . ."

"How old?"

"Sixty, maybe. Or seventy." She hesitated. "Maybe eighty?"

He shook his head. "Mustache? Beard?"

"I don't know."

"Glasses?"

"I don't know."

"Wearing what?"

"I . . . golf clothes, I think, but . . ." She spread her hands.

Torres laughed. "Got it. One basic, garden-variety old geezer; no distinguishing characteristics. Well, I'll look into it." The pad went into his hip pocket. He picked up his hat and stood up once more.

"You never did answer my question," she said, wondering where she was getting the nerve.

"What question was that?"

"Do you think he was murdered?"

She expected him to laugh it off, but he only shook his head wonderingly. "If he was, it was one hell of a murder weapon. How do you kill somebody with a lightning bolt?"

It was the same question she had asked Peg a few hours earlier, but by now she had given it some thought, however primitive. "Maybe . . . maybe you could doctor his umbrella—or his golf club or something—to make it more conductive . . . conducive to lightning, or—or—" But she was out of her element and quickly ran down. "Would something like that be possible?" she asked lamely.

"Beats me," he said. He clapped the hat back on his head, tugging at the deeply curled brim. "Well, lemme go see if I can find your friend." And off he ambled, looking like the guy who'd come to fix the garbage disposal.

Without ever answering her question.

Chapter 12

The Thrifty Owl Motel ("Clean Rooms for the Budget-Minded Traveler") on Los Alamos's Central Avenue was like a breath from the past, the closest thing Lee had seen to Army barracks since her days in the military. Hardly surprising, really, considering that the building dated back to the 1940s, when the federal government had thrown up long rows of military-style housing for the sudden influx of scientists and technicians working on the Manhattan Project. Over the years, subsequent civilian owners had spruced up the outside of the three-story structure, built a lobby of sorts, and even stuck on a restaurant. But the core of the place remained frozen in time, right down to the flimsy green interior walls, the thin carpeting, the fusty smell of the stairways, the lack of elevators.

No doubt most travelers, even budget-minded ones, found it a depressing place, but for Lee it brought back a lot of good memories. Army life had given her a wonderful taste of the travel and adventure she'd hardly dared hope for as a teenager. It had also given her a hefty taste of mind-numbing routine and deadly boredom, but that had simply come with the territory.

A lot like life on the tour, if you thought about it.

"How we doin'?" said the clerk behind the desk, a gum-cracking, enormous woman who substantially overflowed her stool. She had been seated there every time Lee had gone through the lobby, morning or night. "Got a long-distance call for ya." Her silver and turquoise Navajo bracelets jangled as she handed over a folded pink slip.

"Thanks, Marie." She pocketed the slip without looking at it and went to the stairs.

Graham, she thought, with a sudden sensation in her chest that felt like fullness and emptiness at the same time. Who else would be calling her long-distance? She wanted it to be him . . . and yet she wanted it not to be him. She was no closer to knowing what to do about their relationship than she'd been the last time she'd seen him, almost four months earlier. With her heart in her mouth, Lee had asked him to put everything on hold for the rest of the tour season. Then, as now, she'd been torn, knowing that whatever he answered would make her miserable. He'd quietly agreed to it (making her miserable), and since then they'd spoken only three or four times over the telephone and exchanged a couple of stilted, walking-on-eggshells letters.

She knew well enough what the source of the problem was: she'd met him too early. Graham, at thirty, was thinking about settling down and raising a family; Lee wasn't, at least not yet. They'd never had an explicit, down-to-earth discussion about it—intuitively, they'd known enough to steer clear of the subject—but each knew how the other felt. She supposed her reluctance had a lot to do with her being the oldest of a family of six children whose ages stretched over seventeen years. By the time she'd left home at eighteen Lee felt as if she had earned a long, long vacation from dirty diapers, runny noses, and the Terrible Twos. If she never saw another burp cloth it would be too soon.

Five years later she felt exactly the same, if not more so. And she was increasingly aware—and protective—of the stimulus, the challenge, the demands that went with the crazy life she'd chosen. Moreover, she knew her own limitations. Being one of the superwomen, juggling a golf career, husband, and children, was more than she could manage. Sure, a lot of female golfers were married, but as far as Lee could see, the successful marriages seemed to be the ones in which either the husband's occupation was equally bizarre and nomadic, like professional baseball or sports telecasting, or else the husband had quit his own work to manage his wife's career. And she wasn't too sure about the latter.

While Graham Sheldon's police work definitely had its bizarre moments, it was far from transient, and the idea of his quitting his job to run her career was laughable. For one thing, he'd never consider it. For another, what career? The golfers who patronized the Thrifty Owl Motel didn't ordinarily require a great deal of professional assistance in the management of their financial and business affairs.

In her second-floor room, Lee set down the bucket of ice she'd picked up in the lobby, switched on the lamp next to the bolted-down television set, and opened the note. *Sheldon Graham called*, it said, making her laugh. *Pls retn.* And then, with a different pen: *Again.* And finally, underlined: *3 times*.

Well, that took care of one worry anyway. Whenever she heard from him, the first thought that came to mind was that he was telephoning or writing to call the whole thing off. Graham was attractive, sweet, stable, and funny, and God knew that there were plenty of available women in California. Available and predatory. With Lee not staking a formal claim, she was always expecting to hear that he'd finally given up on her and taken up with some female who could be there when he needed her.

But you didn't telephone someone three times in a single day to give her a dear-Jane call.

She made herself a makeshift ice bag from a towel, pulled back the thin chenille bedspread, piled both pillows against the headboard, and stretched out with a sigh. Then she propped her injured arm on another towel and applied the ice.

Comfortably settled, she dialed Graham's number on the old-fashioned black telephone. The X ray had taken less time than expected and she had an hour before Peg's dinner party.

He answered on the second ring.

"Hello?"

"Graham, it's—"

"Lee!" His voice sounded wonderful. "Are you all right?"

"Yes, I'm fine." Considering.

"But I heard you were knocked out of the tournament with an injury. What happened?"

"Really, Graham, it wasn't that terrible. To begin with, it was just a rotten lie. I—"

"You mean it's not true?" he said with obvious relief. "Why would they say on television—"

Her laughter cut him off. It was several seconds before she could stop.

"I'm certainly glad I'm amusing you," he said pleasantly.

"Poor Graham," she said, wiping tears from her eyes. "I can never believe how little you know about golf."

"I tried to learn," he pointed out. "I kept going to sleep."

She explained what had happened to her on the course and how she'd reinjured herself trying to help Ted Guthrie.

Graham was astonished. "The man who was killed by lightning? *You're* the one who found him?"

"Yes, lucky me."

His voice softened. "It must have been pretty awful."

"Well, what hurts is that I'm out of the tournament and I didn't even do him any good. You know, if it was really an accident, I can be philosophical about it. Just a bad break. But, let me tell you, if it turns out some *murderer* ruined my chance at my first big win, I'm going to be—"

"Murderer? Lee, what are you talking about? Why should it be murder? *How* could it be murder?"

"Well, there are a lot of things. When Detective Torres interviewed me, he seemed to think there was something funny—"

"Torres," Graham said. "Torres. Is his first name Ruben?"

"How would I know that? I don't go around calling detectives by their first names. Except for you, of course."

"It has to be Ruben Torres. He was at Oakland with me. That's right, now that I think about it, he left about a year before I did and went out to Arizona or New Mexico or someplace. Long nose, thin, dark—"

"Yes, that's right. And he was wearing a hat with an "A" on it. Is that an Oakland team?"

"Yes," he said, laughing. "I can never believe how little you know about baseball. Lee, did Ruben actually say he thought it was a homicide?"

"No, he didn't come out and say it, but I could tell from his questions that he was suspicious. And *I'm* suspicious too, and so is Peg. I think—"

"Lee. Stop right there. Don't fool around in this thing. Ruben Torres doesn't need your help. Leave it to the police."

"Why, of course. What else would I do?"

"Stay out of it," Graham warned, shifting into his policeman's voice. "I know you, Lee. Don't even think about digging around on your own."

"Honestly, Graham, I'm not."

Well, maybe a little. How could she not? Whoever had

killed Ted Guthrie—if anybody had—had also dealt her the worst blow of her career; she owed the crumb a little something back. Besides, she had the impression that Ruben Torres *could* use her help. Lee had easy access to all kinds of conversations and gossip that the detective didn't. Why shouldn't she keep her ears open and pass along any relevant tidbits she happened to hear?

"All right, then," Graham muttered, sounding far from satisfied.

They had hit a dead spot. With their personal relationship off-limits, it never took long to get to one. "Well, I guess that's about it . . ." one or the other of them would soon say, and then it would be over. Another month or more before she heard his voice.

"I had one bit of good luck today," she said to keep it going.

"Oh?" Graham said, already sounding distant.

She told him about the television job.

"That's wonderful, Lee," he said, "you'll be terrific." But there was something forced about it. Had he been hoping she'd come spend some time in Carmel while her elbow healed?

"Graham . . ." She had an almost uncontrollable urge to tell him she missed him terribly, to tell him how very much she needed him, to ask him if he could possibly get away to spend a few days there with her in New Mexico. He would come if she asked; she was sure he would. And yet, if she did that, what would happen to the balanced, trucelike status quo they'd—

"Yes?" he said.

"Nothing," Lee murmured.

"Oh," he said softly.

There was another long silence.

"Well," Graham said, "I guess that's about it . . ."

92

Chapter 13

". . . another splendiferous day here in the Land of Enchantment, with temperatures expected to soar into the middle—"

With a groan Lee reached out to flick off the clock radio, then cocked one eye open to check the digital numbers: 6:35. Automatically she flexed the fingers of her left hand. The pain was still there but duller now; cooler and more distant. She'd always been a good healer. Maybe she would fool Dr. Harrelson and be back in harness in a couple of weeks, in time for Denver. She yawned, turned over on her back, closed her eyes again and drifted for a few moments.

The immediate question, she thought sleepily, was whether they were going to put TV makeup on her before she started work. Because if they were, what was the point of putting on makeup now? And if she didn't put on makeup she could just lie there until seven, a whole, lovely twenty-five minutes, and still be downstairs in time for the shuttle to the golf course. On the other hand—

The clock radio chirrupped. Grumbling, she banged the snooze button but it only did it again. No, not the radio, the telephone. She heaved onto her side and stretched for it.

"Unnkh?" she said half into the pillow.

Graham's marvelous laugh spilled from the earpiece. "Now what makes me think I woke you up?"

"Graham!" She sat up and brushed hair from her face. "What a surprise—I didn't think I'd hear from you for another month—" She winced. How would he take that? Would he think she meant she didn't *want* to hear from him for another month? *Did* she want to hear from him? How in the world had she let her life get so complicated?

"That's not the only surprise. I have a better one than that. Well, I hope I do." He paused, and then with something uncharacteristically like diffidence, said: "I'm downstairs in the lobby."

That woke her up, but good. "You're *here* . . . *now?*"

"Well, of course, now," he said mildly. "How could it not be now if I'm talking to you on—"

"I mean *why* are you here? *How*—" Again she cut herself off with a grimace. If she kept putting her foot in her mouth he was going to turn around and head back to California, and that would take care of all the complications. Love-life problems solved. There wouldn't be one.

"As long as I happen to be in the neighborhood, do you suppose I might come up and say hello?" he suggested.

"Oh, yes!" she cried. "Come!" At last, she'd said something she meant with her whole heart. "Room 205."

"Be up in a sec."

She lay back against the pillow, bewildered and excited. If someone had asked her a day or two ago how she would react if Graham were to show up on her doorstep in the morning, she would have predicted an obscure jumble of feelings impossible to sort out. But there was nothing obscure about what she felt now. She was *happy*, happier, to tell the truth, than she'd been since she'd seen Graham last, happier—

My God, the room! She threw the cover aside and leaped up dithering, not knowing what to do first. She had done her laundry at Peg's house after last night's party and then gossiped nonstop for almost an hour about the investigation, about Ted Guthrie and the other board members, and about her upcoming work with the television network. As a result she hadn't gotten in until after one o'clock. She'd dumped the laundry on the chair and table, showered, and fallen into bed. Yesterday's clothes were where she'd tossed them on the bureau. A suitcase lay open—open and messy—on the folding rack.

To top it off, there she was goggling unappetizingly back at herself from the mirror, her hair tangled, her face puffy from sleep and creased from the pillow, and her body elegantly decked out in a shapeless, oversized T-shirt that came down to the middle of her thighs and had "Go, Oregon Ducks" emblazoned on the chest.

First things first. She rummaged in the suitcase, not helping matters in there, and came up with a pair of blue shorts that she hastily stepped into. Not that she had any reason to be shy with Graham, technically speaking, but still one didn't receive visitors—

There was his knock, a cheery *tap-tap*.

And suddenly, she *was* shy; shy and a little timid. She froze momentarily, considered quickly doing something about her hair (but what?), and then swallowed her bashfulness, strode to the door, and pulled it open.

"Coffee," he said, holding up a white paper sack.

If anything, he looked worse than she did. He was unshaven, red-eyed, tousled; boyish and haggard both, his sandy hair spiky, his neat mustache bedraggled. And he looked as if he'd been sleeping in his clothes.

He looked, in short, wonderful, and in a moment, barely giving him time to set down the sack, they were locked in each other's arms, swaying gently from side to side, mute and lost in one another.

"How did you get here?" she asked at last, her face nestled in his shoulder, her voice muffled by his windbreaker. "And when? I just talked to you a few hours ago."

"Plane—the red-eye special to Albuquerque, then a car." They were still swaying with their eyes closed, as if slow-dancing with their feet planted. "Fortunately, Daylight Donuts opens at five-thirty, and they let me sit there and swill coffee from then until now."

"Five-thirty?" she said pulling her head back to look into his eyes. "But why didn't you call me then? I have to leave for work in a few minutes. We could have—"

"I figured you could use a good night's sleep," he said, smiling. He touched her forearm, his strong fingers as gentle as goose down. "How's the arm?"

"Not bad, but it's going to take a while. I can feel it, even squeezing toothpaste out of the tube." She had put her head against his shoulder again, but now, smiling, she pushed against him with her hands. "Believe me, I hate to ask this, but you *are* going to let me go eventually, aren't you? It's my first day on the job."

He hugged her once more, then let her go and took his first look around. "So this is the real you," he said, laughing. "The truth will out. Tell me, what was it that exploded in here, the suitcase?"

By now she was in the bathroom brushing her teeth and trying to tug her hair into shape. "Graham," she called, "you know that I couldn't be more happy about your being here, but—" She put her head out through the doorway. "—What the heck are you *doing* here anyway? I thought we agreed . . . well, you know."

"I was worried about you," he said, simply and seriously, looking at her with those clear, candid, blue eyes, "so I came." At that her eyes brimmed. She dashed out to plant one more kiss on his lips, then hurried back into the bathroom.

"Mm, great toothpaste," he said. "Anyway, what with you hurting your arm, and trying to save that guy, and being out of the tournament, and starting a new job, I just thought you could stand some moral support. I know Peg's here and all, but I thought—well, I thought you could use another friend."

"You also thought that if you were here keeping an eye on me, I wouldn't have the nerve to go nosing around about Ted Guthrie's death." She emerged again, dressed, washed, and reasonably coiffed. "Right?"

"That too," he said.

"Graham, how long can you stay? When do you have to go back?" She held her breath, not sure what she wanted him to say.

"Four days. I need to be back on Wednesday."

Apparently that was what she wanted to hear; she felt her shoulders unknot with relief. "That's wonderful," she cried. "We'll have all kinds of time together. And I won't have to work beyond Sunday. We'll have all day Monday and Tuesday to ourselves because I won't have to be at the next tournament until Thursday. Peg says there are ruins nearby and—" She stopped, aware that she was babbling. And that he was studying her with a patient, quizzical expression in his eyes.

"I hope we have some time to talk too," he said quietly. "I'm not sure that a telephone call a month is quite meeting my needs. I think we ought to be able to work out something better."

She nodded. It darn sure wasn't meeting her needs either.

But *was* there something better? She had a queasy feeling that they were going to be a long way apart on what it might be.

"I hope so too," she murmured uneasily.

"Fine," Graham said crisply. "Hey, don't look so gloomy. We'll work it out, I promise you. Now grab your things and I'll drive you to the course." He held up the sack. "There are a couple of apple fritters in here too. You can eat them on the way."

Downstairs, as they crossed the lobby from the hallway, they earned a knowing smirk from Marie, just arranging herself on her stool.

"This is my friend Graham Sheldon," Lee said, speaking with great clarity, "who just arrived from California a few minutes ago."

"Oh, is that so?" Marie said, not quite leering. "Well, how do ya do?"

"Oops," Graham said as they climbed into his rented Ford Escort a few moments later, "there goes your reputation. Sorry about that. Listen, when do I see you next? Are you free for lunch?"

"I doubt it, but I think I'll be getting off about five."

"Okay, I'll pick you up."

"What are you going to do all day, watch the tournament?"

He looked at her as if she'd asked him if he planned to spend the day watching guppies spawn in a tank. "I think I'll give Ruben a call, for one thing, and see if I can get together with him. It's been a while."

She jabbed her finger at him. "Ha, you're going to ask him all about the Ted Guthrie thing, aren't you?"

He shrugged as he pulled out into the traffic. "Conceivably, it might come up."

"Well, how come I'm supposed to leave it to the local

police," she demanded, "but you come barging in from out of town and jump right in?"

"Because," he explained, "I am a seasoned law enforcement officer of impeccable discretion and cunning ability. You, on the other hand, are a mere inexperienced bunny."

It took a moment for her to understand. "That's *rabbit*," she said wryly.

"Rabbit," he agreed. "Where do I pick you up at five?"

"The control truck, I guess. If I'm not there, somebody will be able to tell you where I am. It's the trailer parked behind the clubhouse, next to the garbage dumpsters."

"The trailer behind the clubhouse, next to the garbage dumpsters," he echoed reflectively. "Gosh, I sure hope all this glamour doesn't go to your head."

Chapter 14

"You're asking me," Dr. Scuffey said, paraphrasing Ruben's words with keen interest, "whether it's possible with any certainty to attract lightning to the human body."

"Well, yeah," Ruben said.

"Whether it's possible, for example, by placing a golf club or some other metallic object in the hand during a lightning storm, to divert a nearby discharge of atmospheric potential through the body in question on its way to the earth's mass."

"Well . . . yeah. I think that's what I'm asking."

"Whether, in short, it is possible to utilize lightning as a murder weapon."

Ruben nodded. That's what he was asking, all right.

Dr. Scuffey clasped his hands behind his ginger-haired head and leaned back in his chair, gazing at the ceiling. "Ha," he said. And gave himself over to thought.

Ruben waited patiently, pretending to sip the stale coffee that Dr. Scuffey had gotten him from someplace. It wasn't everywhere, he thought, that you could get stale coffee at eight o'clock in the morning. Not even at LAPD. But then

they were in a scientific establishment, and scientists were
no doubt well above the trivial concerns of ordinary men.

They were deep inside Los Alamos National Laboratory's
Advanced Computing Center, where a cubbyhole of an office, cluttered with printouts and cardboard file cartons, had
been carved out among the humming supercomputers and
superprinters for Dr. Lynton Scuffey, Chief of Atmospheric
Research and, so Ruben had been reliably informed, one of
America's three leading authorities on lightning.

That was one thing about working in Los Alamos; when
you needed a scientist, you never had very far to go.

"Impossible," Dr. Scuffey said, surfacing. "Absolutely,
categorically, unconditionally impossible." He shook his
head firmly, just in case Ruben might have missed his point.
"No ifs, ands, or buts."

Ruben smiled. "Damn, I was hoping you could give me
a definite answer."

"Let me put it this way, Detective. *If* you were to induce
a potential victim to go up to the highest spot around—
higher than nearby buildings, trees, hills—and *if* you were
to ask him to be good enough to stand there during a
thunderstorm holding on to a forty-foot metal pole pointed
straight up, then you might have a . . . oh, a one-in-a-
hundred chance of bringing it off. But your man wasn't in
a high place, was he?

"No, he was in a sort of little valley. But there were
some power lines nearby—"

"Power lines?" Brushlike, ginger eyebrows lifted. "How
high off the ground?"

Ruben called up the scene in his mind. He'd gone there
the previous evening before leaving the golf course. "About
forty feet, maybe."

"Metal pylons or wooden poles?"

"Wooden poles."

"Then no, it's inconceivable that—"

"Look, couldn't the lightning have hit the wires and then bounced down to him? Doesn't that happen sometimes?"

"*Couldn't* it have happened? Yes, of course it could. Apparently it *did* happen. Induced voltage, we call it. But your question to me was: Could it have been engineered, premeditated? And there, I have to tell you that it could not. Erase the possibility from your mind, Detective. Well, well, sorry I couldn't be more helpful."

He rose to shake hands, a man with profounder things to worry about, and turned Ruben over to an assistant to be seen out.

Sure, Ruben thought, starting up his engine. *Erase it from your mind, Detective.* Easy for Scuffey to say, but Scuffey was concerned only with atmospheric phenomena. Scuffey didn't have to worry about a disappearing golf club, or umbrella, or whatever Guthrie had been holding in his hand; Scuffey didn't have to worry about a missing cart or whatever Guthrie had been sitting in or on—if in fact he'd been sitting, and not, as Minkoff had suggested, already lying down when the lightning hit, a possibility that raised even more questions.

And Scuffey certainly didn't know or care that to half the population of Cottonwood Creek Ted Guthrie's demise was more an occasion for merriment than for lamentation.

Chapter 15

Graham sucked gratefully at the double-tall *caffè latte*.
Now who would have thought you could get a first-rate
caffè latte and decent *biscotti* in Los Alamos, New Mexico?
He might have been in Berkeley or Seattle. Even the coffee
house itself would have fit right in on Berkeley's Telegraph
Avenue; a roomy, steamy, unadorned kind of place with
customers who came to stay for a while, with newspapers
scattered on the tables, and with a well-thumbed magazine
rack that sported everything from *Time* and *Newsweek* to
Parabola: The Magazine of Myth and Tradition, *The Indigenous
Woman*, and *The Journal of Holistic Anthropology and Shamanistic Enlightenment*.

Come to think of it, could you really get *The Journal of
Holistic Anthropology and Shamanistic Enlightenment* even in
Berkeley?

Ruben had suggested that they meet at 8:30 A.M. in
the Cafe Allegro downtown, and Graham had passed the
intervening time shaving, showering, and changing clothes
at the Los Alamos Inn (the Thrifty Owl Motel, he had

found, not entirely to his disappointment, was filled to capacity with Lee's fellow rabbits).

When Ruben finally showed up at 8:45 wearing what appeared to be the same A's baseball cap he'd been wearing when last seen three years ago, it was with the air of a man with things on his mind, but he lit up on seeing Graham and for fifteen or twenty minutes they had a good time rehashing the bad old days in Oakland and getting caught up on each other's personal lives. Graham didn't have much to say on that score, but Ruben had had two more children, bringing the total count to four, all of them under eight. That probably went a long way toward explaining the worried look.

"I understand," Graham said once they'd wound down, "that you've got yourself an interesting case."

"What case?"

"The lightning death."

"How do you know about that? I mean, how do you know it's interesting? You want a couple more *biscotti*? You should try the chocolate ones."

Graham shook his head. "Lee Ofsted's my . . ." He hesitated. His what? ". . . my girlfriend," he finished firmly. And hoped it was true. "That's why I'm here."

"No kidding." Ruben took off his cap and ran a hand through what was left of his hair. In three years he had lost quite a bit. "What do you know about that? Pretty. Seems real nice too. Jeez, what does a girl like that see in you?"

Graham was ridiculously pleased. "Must be my salary," he said roughly and changed the subject. "She says you think it's a homicide."

Ruben hunched his skinny shoulders and studied his coffee cup. "I think it's . . . interesting. I just came from talking to this scientist at the lab, and he—" He looked up. "Hey, you know anything about lightning?"

"A little."

"Really? Well, let me tell you what we have, and you tell me what you think."

Twenty minutes later, with a second *latte* comfortably inside him, Graham reached across the table to hand Ruben his cap. "How about driving me over to where it happened? I just might have an idea."

*   *   *

"Right here," Ruben said, standing in the crisp morning sunlight at the edge of a ten-foot-wide swath that had been cut through the pinyon for maintenance of the overhead power lines. Next to it, emerging from a stand of maple trees and running parallel to the swath for ten yards or so, was the gravel track they had driven on from the club parking lot. From the other side of the hill in front of them, they could hear occasional voices and the patter of polite, golf-style applause. The third round of the tournament, not visible from where they stood, was under way.

"Lee was coming from over there in her cart," Ruben said, "and drove past before she realized Guthrie was lying here. Then she ran back and worked like a trouper to revive him, but he was long gone. Like I said . . ."

"Uh-huh," Graham murmured as Ruben went on, "right." But his eyes were on the power lines, not the ground.

"Ruben," he said quietly, "I think I might know what happened here."

Ruben was brought up short. "You might—how could you—you're kidding me."

"I'm serious. And I think you could be right; this wasn't any accident."

"Wait a minute, how the hell—"

"Let's head back to your office. I'll tell you on the way."

Ruben took a last wild look around him, trying in vain

to find whatever it was that Graham had seen. "I don't know, you must be a hell of a lot smarter than me."

Graham smiled. "So what else is new?"

* * *

"This would have been a few months after you left Oakland PD," Graham said as Ruben turned left onto Central Avenue. "There was this suicide down in San Ramon—"

"Suicide! You're not going to tell me this guy killed himself?"

"Just listen, will you? What this guy in San Ramon did was electrocute himself. He stands under a high-voltage line like the one on the golf course, he ties a fifty- or sixty-foot piece of uninsulated electrical wire around his wrist, and he ties the other end to a hammer."

Ruben frowned at him. "A *hammer?*"

"To use as a weight. It could have been anything fairly heavy; a brick, a branch, a broomstick, anything. Then he takes the hammer and flings it over the high-voltage line, trailing the wire. When the wire comes down and falls onto the line—"

"Zap," said Ruben thoughtfully.

"Zap," agreed Graham.

Ruben looked at him as he swung the car into the parking lot behind the police station and guided it into a vacant slot among the row of black police cars. "Just let me get this straight. You're not suggesting Guthrie killed himself, are you?"

"No, of course not. Otherwise—"

"Otherwise the wire would still have been wrapped around his hand when Lee got there."

"That's right," Graham said.

Ruben turned off the ignition and sat quietly for a moment. "But what does this have to do with lightning?"

"Nothing," Graham said. "Except for appearances."

"You think we were *supposed* to think it was a lightning accident?"

Graham shrugged. "Well, it's what you did think, isn't it? Look, I'm not saying this was the only way it could have happened. I'm saying it's worth considering."

Ruben considered it. Graham knew he was a first-rate cop, but his strength lay in his disciplined, one-step-at-a-time approach to policework. He was great at building his cases piece by careful piece; they almost always stood up in court. But conjecture wasn't his forte.

"It's pretty far-fetched, Graham," he said. "I mean, sure, I guess it's possible, but so are a lot of other things. Why would this make any more sense than that he was killed by lightning while he was holding a golf club or something in his hand?"

"The wound," Graham said promptly. "You told me the burn was on his palm and around the first two knuckles. If he was just holding something in his hand, how did the *back* of his hand get burned?"

"I just figured . . . I tell you the truth, I'm not sure what I figured."

"Well, what I figure is that it could be from having a stiff piece of wire coiled around his hand. What do you think?"

Ruben leaned back in the driver's seat, his arms folded. "No, there's a problem with this. Nobody's just going to stand around while someone ties a wire around his hand and then connects him to ten thousand volts of electricity."

"But was he standing? Didn't you say Minkoff told you he might have been lying down at the time of the electrocution? It's possible he was already unconscious."

"From what? Minkoff didn't find any other injuries or drug indications, or anything like that."

"Minkoff didn't do an autopsy. That's why the body went to OMI in Albuquerque, isn't it?"

"True," Ruben admitted, apparently beginning to come around. "Hey, come on in, let me give Albuquerque a call and see what they have to say for themselves. They were gonna autopsy him first thing this morning."

They walked across the parking lot to a squat, featureless, brown building that looked as if it had been constructed to withstand the next nuclear blast (not an inappropriate style for Los Alamos, Graham mused) and into a small lobby in which the concrete-bunker motif was continued: yellow-painted, cinder-block walls and gray institutional carpeting. The only decoration was a row of glass cases with police shoulder patches from around the world. By comparison, it made Carmel's terraced, flower-surrounded police station seem downright prettified.

Boink-boink, *boink-boink-boink*. Ruben punched a keypad beside a metal door to get them into the linoleum-tiled hallway beyond. His "office," like the "offices" of detectives almost everywhere, was a desk and a couple of chairs in a bullpen-like room he shared with three others. Ruben waved hello to a colleague yawning over a crossword puzzle, the only other person in the room, sat Graham down, and looked at the telephone message on his desk.

He held up the note. "They're ahead of us. It's a call from Albuquerque with a preliminary report. Let me call them back."

For the next ten minutes Ruben asked questions, answered them, and sat for long periods with his ear to the receiver, nodding occasionally and making notes with a stubby fountain pen on a yellow pad. For his part Graham fidgeted and sighed, a little surprised to find himself champing at the bit, impatient with Ruben's slow, meticulous note taking. But this was Ruben's case, not his, he reminded himself; there was nothing for him to get impatient about.

And yet it *felt* like his case. There was Lee's traumatic involvement for one thing. For another, assuming his theory was on target, he had practically solved the thing for Ruben, hadn't he? (Well, except for who did it and why, and a few similar little details.) And now, undeniably, he had the policeman's universal urge to see an investigation through, once started.

But it was out of the question. This was Los Alamos, not Carmel. And he was only going to be here a few days. By Wednesday he'd be back—

Ruben hung up the phone at last. "Cause of death looks like cardiopulmonary arrest."

"Standard in electrocution," Graham observed.

"Standard in anything," Ruben said.

So it was, Graham thought. Saying the cause of death was cardiopulmonary arrest was like saying the cause of death was death. "What else?" Graham asked.

"This you're gonna like," Ruben said. "Something hit him—hard—on the side of the head, above and behind the left ear. Minkoff didn't find it because there wasn't any fracture; just a contusion hidden by his hair. But inside they found a massive subdural hematoma."

"Ah. That explains why he didn't put up a fight."

"Right. Someone cracked him over the head first and laid him out. Damn near killed him right there." He capped his pen and slid the tablet over to one side. "Which just leaves one big problem."

"Which is?"

"Remember, you said it couldn't be a suicide because if it was, the wire would still be there, but it wasn't?"

"Sure."

"All right, what happened to it? If it worked the way you think, how'd the guy who killed him get the wire off without getting zapped himself?"

Graham thought he had the answer to that too, but it seemed a time to tread cautiously. As nice a guy as Ruben was, Graham was on his turf, and there was no such thing as a cop who didn't get a little put out when he was edified

109

about his craft by an outlander, even by another cop, and even if by invitation. And Graham had been doing a lot of edifying.

"I remember the way things worked in San Ramon," he said. "That might help."

"So how did things work in San Ramon?" said Ruben, who gave not the slightest indication of being put out.

The power lines in San Ramon, Graham explained, were equipped with fuse protectors that automatically cut off the current if there was a significant increase in resistance. And a human body creating an electrical path to the ground would cause just such an increase. The power would go off immediately (too late, unfortunately, to be of any use to the body in question) and would stay off until a lineman came to check on what the problem was.

"Assuming that Los Alamos County has the same setup," he concluded, "and assuming that the killer went to the trouble of finding out about it, he'd know that once Guthrie was electrocuted, it'd be perfectly safe to take off the wire and get rid of it."

"Yeah," Ruben said, nodding, "so all I have to do now is call County Utilities and find out if there was a power outage on that section of the line yesterday at around two o'clock. If there was, you might be on to something. If there wasn't—"

"Then I'm all wet," Graham admitted. And you have to come up with a theory on your own, he added silently.

Ruben found the number in his telephone book, dialed, was twice referred, and finally got to ask his question.

"Yeah, I'll wait," he said into the receiver. "Listen, Graham, when do you go back?"

"Wednesday, why?"

"Well, I was thinking. If this is really a homicide, I've got a hell of a problem on my hands. I mean, that golf course is full of people I can't hold in town. I've got to get some leads fast."

"I guess you do."

"So I was hoping you might, well . . ."

"Work with you?" Graham asked hopefully.

"I'm not talking about getting you detailed here, you understand, just a little unofficial help. Your girlfriend gives you an in with these people that I don't have. Besides, I know *frijoles* about golf, and that could turn out to be a problem. But you must know all about it, right?"

Graham hesitated while an internal dialogue, brief but heated, took place between his native honesty and his interest in the case.

"Well, yes, a little, sure," he admitted.

"That's what I figured. So maybe—if you're interested, I mean—you could help me out with some of the—" He brought the receiver back to his ear and held up his hand. "Yeah, I'm still here."

"Thank you very much," he said after listening, then gently replaced the receiver.

"Power was interrupted in that sector at one-fifty-one P.M. yesterday due to what they call a 'fault current'—a large change in resistance. It was turned on again at three-oh-five, when a lineman couldn't find anything wrong with the system. They assume it had something to do with the lightning. Some kind of fluke."

Gratified, Graham sat back. "There you are then."

Ruben nodded thoughtfully, stroking his prominent nose with thumb and forefinger.

"I'll be damned," he said. "What'll they think of next?"

Chapter 16

"Chiles rellenos, extra flour tortillas, order of black beans," Boyd said into the telephone, reading aloud from a penciled list in his notebook. "That's *black* beans, not refried. Yesterday you sent over refried by mistake . . . no, I didn't ask for refried yesterday, I definitely asked for black, I always ask for black. Look, I have it written down right here . . ." He thumbed back a couple of pages. "Definite- ly . . . well, look, it's no big deal, just make sure they're black today, okay? Oh, and plenty of the green salsa, the hot kind . . ."

He put his hand over the mouthpiece and smiled at Lee. "Sure you haven't changed your mind? These people make the best Mexican food in Los Alamos, and you don't really want to eat the stuff you get in the mess tent, believe me. CBS we're not."

Lee shook her head with conviction. "Thanks, no, I'm not hungry."

Two and a half hours into her new job, she was too keyed up to eat anything, let alone stuffed green peppers, at ten in the morning. She had been on the tour long enough to know that televising golf was hardly a restful occupation, but the frantic activity, the mind-boggling number of technicians and assistants and "ancillaries" (of which Lee learned that she was one), and the unrelenting pandemonium that she'd encountered that morning had bowled her over all the same. These people seemed to thrive at a level of tension, commotion, and seeming anarchy that made her helter-skelter life on the tour seem as tidy and well regulated as a job at the local bank.

Boyd had given her a whirlwind overview of the overall process, introduced her to a preoccupied Mike Bulger and a few others, and then unceremoniously plopped her in front of a camera at the driving range to interview Jane Silberberg, currently tied for third. No rehearsal, no warm-up.

No makeup, either. She would probably get an anxious call from her mother this evening asking why she looked so washed out; what had happened to the color in her cheeks? Was her elbow hurting her? (It wasn't.)

Worst was the headset she'd had to wear, with its IFB—"interruptible feedback" feature—the apparent purpose of which was to allow unseen people in the truck to shout incoherent or contradictory instructions simultaneously into her right and left ears while she tried to listen to Jane's answers and frame her own questions at the same time. Fortunately, the session had been taped, not live, or she probably would have lost her job right there. As it was, it had needed five takes to get it right, by which time she was dripping with sweat and wondering if it might not be easier after all to try getting back on the tour with a one-handed golf swing.

Boyd took his hand from the mouthpiece. "Oh, and some of those good green chiles, and that's it. Right, the usual place. I'll have somebody waiting."

He folded his telephone and slipped it back into one of the multitude of pockets in his safari-style vest (no wonder it was almost a uniform with the television people), and unhooked a two-way radio from his belt.

"Lou," he said into it, and waited. "Lou, I can't hear you, Lou. You have to press the send button. Remember? Look down near the bottom, on the left. You'll see a big gray . . . There you go, that's better. Lou, they're going to be delivering my breakfast to the gatehouse in fifteen minutes. It'll have my name on the box. Take it over to the mess tent for me, will you? Put it on the execs' table, the big one in the back. Go ahead and pay with the twenty I gave you."

The radio crackled brokenly in response.

"Don't worry about it. Buy yourself a beer or something with the change. After work, of course."

Another crackle. Lee couldn't recognize the words, but she recognized Lou's indignant tone; she'd heard it often enough.

"Sorry, sorry," Boyd said. "No offense. All right, sure, you can give it back to me at the end of the day, how's that?"

He hooked the radio back on his belt, laughing. "One of a kind, that guy. Where'd you ever find him?"

"I think he found me," Lee said. "Fortunately."

They were enjoying the relative peace of the open space in front of the control truck. Normally a clubhouse staff parking area, it was now a snarl of black, blue, gray, and green cables, shiny metal trunks, and wooden crates stenciled with incomprehensible legends. The one Lee was sitting on said "RTS PLS KIT." Boyd sat across from her on one marked "RT SW CABLES."

"So where were we?" he asked, leaning comfortably back on one elbow. As he'd been yesterday, he was like a solid, stable island in an ocean of wild confusion; calm, sane, and cheerfully long-suffering. "Oh, yeah. Now, after the food break, we'll be doing what we call a FAX check—"

The pocket with the telephone twittered. With a sigh, Boyd dug the instrument out. Lee could hear a shrill yapping coming from it. "No, Mike, of course that's not what we're supposed to be getting," Boyd said patiently when he could fit in a few words. "No, I don't know where he got an idea like that. Look, Mike . . . Mike . . . Mike . . . why don't I just go over and take care of it right now?" The yapping moderated slightly. "Right, don't worry, Mike, there's plenty of time, I'll get it all straightened out."

"Problems?" Lee asked sympathetically as Boyd folded the phone and replaced it.

"Oh, nothing too terrible," Boyd said. "F-14—that's the camera tower on the fourteenth fairway—is mounted too low to see over a little rise, and it can't pick up the golfers from the knees down."

"So what will you do?"

"I'll see when I get there. Either move the tower or have it built up another few feet."

"And is there really time enough to do that?"

"Oh, hell, of course there's time," Boyd grumbled. It was the first time she'd heard him sound even a little grouchy. "Mike's just one of these people who . . . I mean, if he'd just *talk* sometimes instead of screaming, if he'd just assume other people have brains and feelings too . . ." He smiled wearily, the good humor returning to his eyes. "You know what? I think I'm getting too old for this. It's a young man's game."

From what Lee had observed so far, he was right. Other than Boyd's, there wasn't a single gray head among the production people. Most were in their thirties. "What happens to older people in television?" she'd asked Mike earlier, trying to make polite conversation. "Everybody in the truck is young."

"Who knows?" he'd said abstractedly. "The ones that don't get heart attacks get kicked upstairs, I guess."

"Fortunately," Boyd said now, "I'm one of the old crocks who's getting kicked upstairs, and, let me tell you, it's looking better and better."

"You're being promoted?"

"Yeah, as of next fall I'll be ASN's vice-president for golf," he said off-handedly, but she could see the pleasure in his face. "Far removed from the lowly hassles of production."

"Congratulations," she said warmly. Then, after a moment: "What's ASN?"

He stood up, laughing. "The American Sports Network. Your employer. Look, I have to get over to the tower for a few minutes, and I want you to go stoke up with some food at the mess tent even if you're not hungry. It's the last you'll get until five. I'll catch up with you there."

"Here," Lee said, "you're forgetting your notebook."

He took it from her with a grin and a sigh. "Not only am I getting old," he said, "I'm getting absentminded."

* * *

Merely surveying the buffet tables in the tent was enough to bring Lee's appetite galloping back. Of necessity an expert in the scrounging of freebie meals on the road, she rated ASN's staff breakfast a solid nine on a scale of ten. She was suddenly starving, the apple fritter that had been sitting so uneasily in her stomach during the interview with Jane now only a distant memory. If ASN was so inferior to CBS, she thought, shamelessly heaping her tray with half a grapefruit, French toast, sausage, sauteed potatoes, scrambled eggs, and two cartons of milk, then she would certainly make sure she never passed up an opportunity to eat at the CBS mess tent. It would take an awful lot of meals like this before she would find it necessary to order food from outside. But then, Boyd had had an awful lot of meals like this, so maybe it was understandable.

Not surprisingly, most of the round white tables were

crowded with staffers shoveling in food from plates piled even higher than hers; at the energy level at which they operated, they needed it. What did surprise her, however, was the sight of Peg Fiske breakfasting with the remaining members of the Cottonwood Creek board: Frank Ayala and Vernon Beal, whom Lee had met at Peg's party the previous night, and Dr. Harrelson, the orthopedic surgeon. Lee headed for them.

"What happened yesterday was tragic, absolutely tragic," Vernon was declaiming with every appearance of satisfaction, "but while I am hardly the sort of person to say 'I told you so,' in this instance I feel justified in recalling to your attention my apprehensions—"

"Hi, Lee," a somewhat glazed-eyed Peg said, catching sight of her. "Come join us." She patted the empty seat next to her. "How's life with ASN?"

"A little more hectic than I thought," Lee said, setting her tray down, "but I think I'm going to survive. But what are you all doing here?"

"Boyd Marriner's considering doing a feature on the travails of putting on your first golf tournament," Harry Harrelson said brightly, looking up from his cantaloupe. "He suggested we meet him here for breakfast to talk about it." He held up the plastic-coated card clipped to his shirt pocket. "And provided the passes to get us in. It's quite exciting, I must say." He lowered his voice. "Don't turn around, but there's Skip Cochrane, right over there."

"If it's travails he wants," Frank Ayala said curtly, "he's come to the right place."

"Amen to that," said Vernon, whose lips compressed even more than usual when he caught sight of Lee. "How nice to see you again," he said austerely.

Unfortunately, Lee had put her foot in her mouth at Peg's party the night before. Vernon had seemed vaguely familiar to her from the beginning, but it was two hours before she abruptly remembered where she'd seen him, and when she did she dropped the canapé she was holding onto Peg's cream-colored carpet and brought every conversation within ten feet to a dead stop by pointing her finger at him and blurting: "*You're* the garden-variety old geezer!"

Well, she'd had two glasses of wine, which was two more than she was used to, and it had been an exhausting day, and she probably shouldn't have been at a late-night party in the first place.

Vernon had taken it surprisingly well. "I beg your pardon?" he had murmured with no more than an understandable coolness in his voice.

"The man with the umbrella . . ." Lee had stammered, "the man who went for help . . ."

"Well, of course I am," Vernon had said. "I assumed you remembered."

Vernon, it turned out, had behaved in an entirely unsuspect manner, going directly to the medics with word of the emergency, unhesitatingly giving them his name, and then submitting to an interview with Ruben Torres not long after her own talk with the detective.

He had been relatively magnanimous about being called an old geezer ("What I do resent is the 'garden-variety' part," he had said with a rather labored chuckle), but Lee was not under the impression that she'd made a new friend.

She was arranging her breakfast plates on the table—the tray was loaded to capacity and then some—when Boyd came up behind her.

"Good Lord," he said, laughing, "I'd love to see what you eat when you're hungry."

She colored. "I guess I got a little carried away."

"No, no," he said, clapping a friendly hand on her shoulder, "tuck in, you'll need it." He nodded to the others at the table. "And I'm glad to see the rest of you made it. Hope you're enjoying breakfast."

There were murmurs of assent.

"Let me get my food from the execs' table and I'll join you. I'll just be a minute; I need to set our producer's mind at rest with the latest crisis-intervention report."

"He seems like a pleasant sort," Harry said as Boyd went to the other table, about twenty feet away.

"Extremely," Lee said sincerely, tucking with pleasure into the scrambled eggs.

It was quickly apparent that Boyd was going to be more than a minute or two. Mike was reacting to his report with his usual combination of consternation and peevishness, a few anguished words of which made it back to them.

"That's not the point, goddammit, you shouldn't *have* to explain it to him . . . What does he think he's being paid to do . . . ? Where do we get these people . . . ?"

Boyd made a few soothing gestures without visible result, then sat resignedly down beside him, opening his boxed meal and picking at the cooling contents while he patiently waited for Mike to run down enough to let him get in a word or two.

"Now where was I?" Vernon asked, turning his attention back to their own table.

"As long as we're all together," Peg cut in quickly, "maybe we ought to talk about filling in for Ted on his committee assignments. I'd be willing—"

She was interrupted by a commotion from the direction of the executives' table: a desperate, sucking gasp for air, as if someone had had the wind knocked out of him. Lee saw Boyd, with his back to her, jerk halfway out of his chair, clutch at his throat, and then stumble one step back and go down, taking his chair and a loaded tray table with him. Her line of sight was blocked by the people at an intermediate table, but she heard his body hit the close-cropped lawn that served as a floor; it seemed to her she could feel the horrible thump in her bones.

She caught a glimpse of Mike Bulger and Bonnie Harlow, the people who had been sitting on either side of Boyd. They had both jumped from their chairs and were staring down at him with white, horrified faces. Mike's eyes were popping; Bonnie's short hair was literally standing on end, as if an electric charge had passed through it.

The buzz and clink of convivial eating had come to a sudden, jolting stop with the gasp; everyone in the tent had frozen in mid-movement. Utensils hung motionless over plates or halfway to mouths. Mouths remained open or closed, depending on whether they had been caught talking or chewing. But now everybody came alive at once. Many stood to see better. Excited questions hummed throughout the tent. *What happened? . . . Who was that? . . . Did you see what happened? . . .*

Lee sat motionless, seized in a strange, blank calm; except for the shrinking, twisting sensation in her chest, it was as if she'd been anesthetized, sedated. This couldn't be happening. Somehow, she was certain Boyd was dead and yet she seemed unable to process what it meant, unable even to take an interest. It couldn't be happening.

"Is there a doctor anywhere?" someone at the execs' table was calling, but Harry, hopping from his chair with startling swiftness for all his comfortable plumpness, was already there. She saw his head disappear as he knelt, she heard him demand more room, more air. People hurriedly complied, shifting chairs and tables.

"Ambulance!" he barked. "Call 911!" Someone ran off to do it.

Lee must have been in more of stupor than she realized, because it seemed to her the medical attendants were there in seconds. They were a different pair than the day before, a stone-faced young man and woman in white, and yet there was an uncanny sense that the same events were playing out all over again. The same fishing-tackle box, the same electrodes . . .

Another uncertain passage of time, and Harry rose, his pink scalp shining with sweat. At the raising of his hand, the excited whispering stopped.

"I don't think anyone should leave," he said, "until the police arrive."

The whispering resumed, turned up a notch. "Is he dead?" someone asked, but Harry didn't answer. He talked briefly to the medics, then made his way back and sat heavily, angrily, down in his chair. On the table he placed a meal-sized Styrofoam food carton, letting his forearm rest on it. Lee saw the penciled lettering on the top: "Boyd."

"*Is* he dead?" Peg asked quietly after a moment.

Don't listen, Lee told herself. *If you don't hear him say it, it isn't really true.*

She heard anyway. "Oh, yes," Harry said tiredly, pouring himself a fresh cup of coffee from the pitcher. He did it with one hand, keeping the other wrist on the carton. "He's dead, all right."

"Heart attack?" Frank Ayala asked.

"No, I don't believe so." Harry looked at them with his round, mild blue eyes. "Something he ate, I think. Or drank."

Vernon sat up abruptly. "Something he *ate*? He stared with horror at what was left of his minced ham and eggs, then back up at Harry. His hand crept reluctantly to his own abdomen. "Ptomaine?"

Harry shook his head. "I believe he was poisoned," he said without expression, although his arm settled more protectively still on the food carton. "Possibly a neurotoxin of some sort, such as strychnine, or perhaps an alkaloid or anticholinergic—Lee, are you all right?"

She wasn't all right. The self-willed daze she'd been in

had snapped at last. She was hunched over the table, her forehead resting against her crossed forearms. "Oh, God," she was murmuring, "oh, God."

And on the backs of her hands her tears ran hot and wet.

Chapter 17

"Drink it," Peg commanded.

Lee looked sullenly at the steaming mug. "What is it?"

"Tea—two bags—with two teaspoons of Coffee-mate and three teaspoons of sugar."

"Ugh."

"Trust me. It got me through six months of late-night MBA casework." She pushed the mug closer. "Now drink."

Lee took a tentative sip, then smiled wanly. "It's a little sweet." She had another, longer gulp. Peg was right; she felt her strength flow back in a slow wave, her drooping spirit begin to perk up. "What's happening out there?"

While the other forty or so people who had been in the ASN mess tent were milling restlessly in the clubhouse lounge, where Ruben Torres and two uniformed officers were interviewing them one by one, Peg, seeing how shaken Lee was, had used her "command presence" to appropriate the nearby boardroom for the two of them to wait their turns.

Now she sank comfortably into one of the padded swivel chairs at the table and drank some of her coffee. "It'd be hilarious if it wasn't so awful," she said. "With network airtime coming up fast, the TV types are alternating between hysterics, power plays, and temper tantrums, trying to tri-age themselves—to work out who gets interviewed when, so they can get back to work. But they're not having much success agreeing."

"Why am I not surprised?" Lee muttered.

"From a business management perspective, I'd have to say their nonprogrammed decision-making process leaves something to be desired. Yelling seems to be the preferred mode."

Lee nodded, reviving by the second. "From what I've seen so far, they tend to be a pretty excitable bunch even when nothing's wrong. Except for Boyd." She toyed with the mug, slowly shaking her head back and forth. "He was like a rock. And he was kind too. He didn't really need me for this tournament, you know—or Lou either. He was just trying to help us . . ." Her voice trailed away. "Sorry about losing it back there."

"Don't be ridiculous," Peg said dismissively. "Who wouldn't lose it after everything you've been through in the last two days? Besides, you didn't lose it, you just, well—"

"The thing is, what I was feeling wasn't really grief or—or sorrow so much, it was more like—" She stopped, not sure what it was more like.

"Anger," Peg said.

Lee considered. "Yes, anger. Rage. He was a really decent person, Peg, the one person I . . . and somebody puts poison in his—his chiles rellenos . . . damn it, I just feel . . . I just wish I could—"

"Now wait a minute, Lee," Peg said reasonably. "We don't really know that anyone *killed* him. There haven't been any lab tests yet. Maybe Harry made a mistake. He's an orthopedic surgeon, what does he know about poison?"

Lee lifted an eyebrow. "Do you really believe that?"

"No, of course not. I'm just trying to calm you down."

"Well, I'm calm," Lee said, "but I wish there was something I could *do*."

"So do I," Peg said. She hunched her shoulders. "But what? Oh, by the way, guess who's out there."

"Who?"

"Graham. He says he'll stop in and say hello as soon as he can."

Lee perked up another notch. "What's Graham doing here?"

"I don't know. He was with Ruben."

"What—" She brushed her hair from her face. "Oh, God, I must look like a mess. Every time he shows up I'm— Peg, lend me a mirror."

"I should only look like you do when you're a mess," Peg grumbled, and at that moment Graham quietly opened the door and came in, shaved and handsome and rested-looking in a tan denim jacket and jeans.

"It's sure nice to be in peaceful little Los Alamos," he said. "Hi, Peg." He took a long, searching look at Lee, then came to her, knelt down beside her chair, and wordlessly wrapped his arms around her.

It was just what she needed. She hugged him back as hard as she could.

"Oh, well," Peg sang out to no one, "I guess I can go find something to do somewhere—"

They separated, laughing. "He's just giving me a little moral support," Lee said.

"That's what I'm here for," Graham agreed.

"Graham, what *are* you here for?" Lee asked. "I mean, right here, right now."

"You keep asking me that. It's a good thing I'm not sensitive." He got up off his knees and propped himself on the edge of the table. "I'm working with Ruben, more or

125

less. I was with him in his office when the call came about Marriner's death. He asked me if I wanted to come along. He doesn't know much about golf and he thought maybe I could explain things if he needs it."

Lee was too dumbfounded by this statement to reply, and it was Peg who spoke next.

"Graham, do they know for sure if Boyd was poisoned yet?"

"He was poisoned, all right. OMI still has to get back to Ruben on the blood samples, but there isn't much doubt about it."

"Murder," Lee said softly, feeling the hairs rise on the back of her neck. "Someone actually killed him."

"That's right. That makes two." He paused. "Guthrie was murdered too."

"Guthrie—" Lee and Peg exclaimed together.

Graham nodded. "You two were right on target. That wasn't any freak accident." Briefly, he explained the details.

"That is *weird*," Peg said. "What kind of way is that to kill someone?"

"Pretty effective," Graham said. "And damn tricky too. We still wouldn't be any the wiser if not for some first-rate police work. Brilliant, really."

"I think," Peg said dryly, "that means he figured it out himself."

Graham maintained a modest silence.

"Two murders in two days," Peg said. "They have to be connected."

"Oh, I think so. I'd be pretty surprised if we've got more than one murderer. Not that there's any evidence one way or the other."

"This is horrible," Lee said. "Are there any leads? Do you have any suspects?"

"Sure, about four thousand. Any suggestions?"

"Well, the roomful of people out there, to begin with,"

Peg put in. "Especially the people that were sitting with him. I'd think they'd be right at the top of your list."

"It wasn't Mike and it wasn't Bonnie," Lee said, "I can tell you that. I saw their faces when Boyd . . . when it happened."

"And?" Peg said.

"They looked the way I felt—sick . . . shocked . . ."

"That doesn't prove anything. People can put on an act when they know other people are watching," Peg said.

Lee shook her head. "This wasn't any act."

"Maybe they're better actors than you think," Peg persisted. "Or maybe they really *were* horrified. So what? That doesn't mean that one of them couldn't have killed him. We're not talking about some professional hit man here. If somebody at that table poisoned Boyd, why *wouldn't* they look horrified when it actually happened? And sick too? I'd have been looking pretty sick about then if it was me."

"Maybe," Lee said uncertainly.

"Well, what do you think, Graham?" Peg asked.

"It's certainly nice of you to include me in on this," Graham said with a smile. "The fact is, I think you have a good point, Peg—"

"Ha," she said with a glance at Lee.

"—but—"

"But. I should have known."

"—if you were poisoning somebody and hoping to get away with it, would you be sitting right next to him when it actually happened, if you could help it?"

"I guess not," Peg admitted.

"Neither would I. I wouldn't even be in the same room with him. And we know that the food was sitting on the table for a while before he got there so there was time to doctor it and to leave. We're pretty sure that's when it was done. Unfortunately, nobody knows exactly how long it was there. We know the Casa Rosita delivered it to the gatehouse at about ten-fifteen, as usual, and we also know that the guy who picked it up wasn't the same one who's been doing it the last few mornings, so that's an interesting point right there. Unfortunately nobody seems to know *who* he was, but at least we have a description."

"Short," Lee said, "dark, wrinkled, kind of a permanent scowl—"

Graham blinked. "How do you know?"

"It was Lou."

"Lou, your caddie?"

She nodded. "He's working for ASN as a runner. I was there when Boyd asked him to pick it up."

"Terrific," Graham said. "What's his last name?"

To her embarrassment, Lee had to think. Lou had caddied for her more than a dozen times now, and in their own peculiar way they were close, but caddies of Lou's vanishing type were a strange breed; most had pasts as drifters or worse, and they tended to be a little vague as to names. Many weren't known by their real given names at all, but by nicknames: Skooter, Skeeter, Wizard, Porky, Jumbo.

"Sapio," she said at last. "Lou Sapio. I saw him in the tent having breakfast with the other runners. He must be out there in the lounge waiting to be interviewed."

"Great, I'll tell Ruben. There's a press conference set up for 2:30. He'll be glad to get a chance to talk to Lou before then."

"A press conference?" Peg said. "About the murders? Both murders?"

"Yes, why so surprised?"

"But nobody knows Ted's death was murder yet, right? Everyone assumes it was an accident. If you go out and announce it to the world, won't that just put the killer on guard, make him more careful? I'd have thought you'd want to keep it to yourselves for a while."

"Sure, that'd be great, but unfortunately we can't get

away with that anymore. This place is crawling with reporters, and Ruben's going to have to say something. Anyway,
now with what happened to Marriner, everybody's speculat-
ing like mad about Guthrie. But Ruben's not going to
tell everything he knows; only that there are some signs
suggestive of foul play and he's looking into it, and the
D.A. will tell them more in a few days; something like
that."

He got up from the table. "I guess I'd better go back
out there and see if we can run down Lou."

"Graham . . . one thing," Lee said. "Lou's sort of, well,
a little rough around the edges, but don't be misled. Really,
he's—"

"I know," Graham said, laughing, "a sweetheart, wouldn't
hurt a fly. Look, don't worry, I don't think he killed anybody.
I've seen Lou in action. He may be a little odd, but he's no
dummy. He wouldn't be stupid enough to do something that
could be traced back to him as easily as this. But he might
be able to tell us something about—"

At that point, one of the uniformed officers poked his
head into the boardroom. "Lieutenant? Could you come on
back out? Detective Torres'd like to talk with you."

"Be right there, Ron. I have something to tell him too."
He took Lee's hand. "You okay?"

She smiled up at him. "Fine."

He let go of her hand and went to the door. "Pick you
up at five, right?"

"Right. And Graham?"

He looked inquiringly back at her.

"I'm awfully glad you're here."

Chapter 18

"To borrow a phrase from Vernon," Peg said as the door closed behind Graham, "I have just one thing to say on this subject."

"Which is?"

"If the Los Alamos Police Department is getting its golf expertise from Graham Sheldon, then they're in big trouble. Unless Graham's learned an awful lot since the last time I saw him."

Lee shook her head with a smile. "Not a blessed thing." She poured some coffee into her cup from the carafe on the table.

"I could make you some more of that super-tea," Peg offered.

"Thanks all the same, I'm okay now." She swallowed some of the lukewarm coffee. After the hypersweetened tea it tasted like dishwater, a modest improvement. "You know, that's not the only reason the police are in trouble," she said, rotating the cup in her hands. "Think about the time element. It's already Saturday. Tomorrow night everybody connected with this thing starts taking off—everybody who doesn't live here, that is—and then how is Ruben going to get anywhere, when the people he needs to talk to are scattered all over the United States?"

"All over the world," Peg said. "A lot of the golfing crowd goes over for the European tour. You're right, Lee. If Ruben can't get somewhere definite this weekend, I don't see how he's going to have a chance later on."

They were silent for a few moments, each with her own thoughts. "Boyd Marriner went out of his way to help me," Lee said. "He was kind to me. I feel as if I owe him something." She shook her head helplessly. "I hate thinking his murderer might get away with it. I keep trying to think of some way I could help, something I could do."

And Boyd wasn't the only one to whom she owed something. What about the killer himself, the person who hadn't only poisoned Boyd but had, in effect, knocked Lee out of the most gloriously played tournament of her life by electrocuting Ted Guthrie and leaving him there for her to stumble on and try to revive, emphatically wrecking any chance she had of getting back into the contest? He—or she—had some payback coming too, and if there was any possible way of helping to make it, Lee was all for it. With interest.

But what was there that she could conceivably do?

"You know," Peg said thoughtfully, "there just might be something *I* could do. I liked Boyd too. I don't want to see this lousy murderer get away with it either."

"Like what?"

"Well, I was thinking. I might be able to do a little digging around about Ted. Because, as Graham said, there must be a connection between—"

"Slow down, Peg. Now that I think about it, why are we all so sure of that? Even Graham said there's no evidence for it. Are we jumping to conclusions?"

"*Puh-leeze,*" Peg said scornfully, "give me a break. Two

important people involved with the same tournament are murdered on the same golf course inside of twenty-four hours, and they're not related? What do you think, we have daily murders here at Cottonwood? Of course they're related."

"I know, I know," Lee sighed. "I guess I'm playing devil's advocate, just trying to keep us objective."

Peg drew herself up. "*I* am always objective, my dear."

"Of course," Lee said with a smile. "Sorry, I don't know what I was thinking of. All right, what exactly could you do?"

"For starters, I might pay a sympathy call on Myrna Guthrie—that's Ted's wife—and see if it leads anywhere."

"Where could it possibly lead?"

"I don't know; maybe nowhere." Peg raised an eyebrow. "Or maybe I could find out something useful."

"Maybe, but the police are certain to talk to her. What would be the point of your doing it too?"

"The point is, Myrna and I are friends—well, sort of—despite her husband's being such a pain in the—" She bit her lip. "I guess I ought to stop talking about him like that now that he's dead, but, Lord, was it ever true. Anyway, Myrna's kind of a prim, proper person. She'd be much more open with me than with some cop she doesn't know."

At that moment a uniformed policeman poked his head into the boardroom.

"Miss Ofsted? Could we get your statement now?"

"Of course. Is it going to take long? I'm supposed to be at work in less than an hour."

He shook his head. "Nah, they've been running about five minutes. Unless you know something nobody else knows."

"I wish I did," she said, moving toward the door.

At the doorway she turned around. "Um, Peg? Assuming I can get away, do you suppose I could go along with you on that sympathy call?"

Peg grinned back at her. "Well, of course. It never occurred to me that you wouldn't."

* * *

Lee stood irresolutely at the bottom of the five metal steps
leading up to the Inner Sanctum—the shiny, white, fifty-
foot-long trailer known as the control truck or more simply
as The Truck. There was less than an hour until airtime at
one o'clock, and she still had no idea of what she was
expected to do. She had placed a call to Mike Bulger after
the police interview (which had taken only four minutes;
she simply had nothing to tell Ruben other than that Boyd's
meal had been delivered by a local restaurant and picked
up at the gate by Lou, which he already knew), and Mike
had muttered something about getting right back to her.
Indeed, one of his assistants had called her at the clubhouse
a few minutes later, but only to ask if she knew where Lou
was, because there were a hundred things for him to do.

She had obligingly tracked Lou down and continued to
wait by the telephone, but no call had come. It was time
to beard the lion in his den. She raised her hand to knock
at the door of the trailer, then remembered that she was an
ASN staff member and not a visitor, pulled the door open,
and walked in.

The interior was in its usual disarray. The floor was lit-
tered with crumpled paper that had apparently missed the
wastepaper baskets, and the surfaces of the several rows of
narrow tables were cluttered with charts, white Styrofoam
cups (many with pieces chewed out of them) and red Jolt
("Twice the Caffeine") Cola cans. Twenty-two of the twenty-
six various-sized monitors that made up the front wall were
on, some in color, some in black and white, some showing
the early golfers out on the course, some showing color
patterns, some showing a tennis match. And one in the
corner showing a talk show with a heavy, bearded young

man on screen and a caption that said *Says he lost his wife in a bet*. The young man looked vaguely miffed about it.

Most of the people at the tables were shouting instructions at unseen camera operators over the microphones on their headsets. "Great, great, milk it, milk it, stay with that goofy expression on her face!" "Deb, stay with Gunderson on thirteen, stay, stay—ah, too late, dammit, the hell with it." "Bernie, we can edit later. Just work it till it's done, all right, for Pete's sake?"

Others were exhorting the golfers, who mercifully couldn't hear them. "Give us something, give us something," one of the technicians pleaded with Olga Gronski, who was trying for a long putt on the third green, but was short by two feet. The disgusted technician thumped the table with his fist. "You bum, you turkey!"

Mike Bulger, on a stool in the rear, was yelling into his own microphone. "No, I already told you; stay with Torresdahl and Hanson. We need all the footage we can get for the early-round wrap-up." He glanced up, squinting directly at her through the smoke from his own cigarette, but Lee doubted that he was aware that she was there. "No, dammit, N-O! You're not paid to think, Marty, just do it!"

He took off the headset and rubbed a hand over his head, massaging as he went. Apparently he'd been doing it a lot, because his stiff black hair stood out in bushy clumps. "Jesus," he said to the ceiling.

Mike Bulger was a spreading, froglike man in his middle thirties, with a low forehead, a pushed-in, squashed-up face, and a perpetual squint that ran its own small gamut of emotions from strained disbelief to wouldn't-you-know-it frustration. He reached absently for the half-filled Styrofoam cup at his elbow and grimaced when he swallowed; more out of habit than conviction, Lee thought.

It was as good a time as any to interrupt. "I'm terribly sorry about Boyd," she said, going up to him.

Slumped wearily on his stool, he looked at her without interest. "Bummer. Something I can do for you?"

Did he even know who she was? "It must be making things awfully difficult. I know—"

"Burn it!" he shouted in answer to a question from a technician at the front of the room. "Burn it, who needs the damn thing?" His glance came back to her, impatient now.

"I'm Lee Ofsted, Mr. Bulger. Boyd Marriner—"

"I know, I know. Look, can it wait? Just sit in a corner or something. We're on in fifty minutes, we're way behind, the cops are still hassling my people, and I don't know what the hell I'm supposed to do first."

"I don't know what *I'm* supposed to do either," Lee said, sharply, her irritation getting the better of her. "I'm sorry if that's a bummer too, but Boyd died before he finished walking me through my job."

Mike closed his eyes, blew air out of his mouth, and tugged at another tussock of hair. "Look, Lynn—"

"Lee," she said between gritted teeth.

"Look, Lee, I don't have time for this."

"I don't either, Mr. Bulger. Why don't we just call it quits? I'm not sure I'm cut out for this."

That was putting it mildly. A day or two of this and she'd be pulling out her hair too. Figuring out how she was going to make ends meet for the next month would prove to be an interesting problem, but whatever it was had to be better than this. She had her self-respect to think about too. She was like Lou in that respect: she didn't take money for nothing.

"No, don't get excited. Look, we really do need a replacement for Cooper, especially next week for Denver. It's just today that's a problem, okay?" He looked around the trailer as if expecting to find a task she could handle for the moment, but apparently nothing jumped out at him. "I know what," he said, seized with inspiration. "Go ask Skip. I think he's still in the Green Room."

"Skip Cochrane?"

"Right, he's been at this for ten years, he knows the ropes. Tell him I sent you. He'll have tons of stuff for you to do."

Chapter 19

He had nothing for her to do.

"I'd really like to help you out," he said, flashing that famous Hoosier-boy grin, "but, good grief, it's all I can do to figure out what *I'm* supposed to do now. I just can't take on a trainee, not now." He rocked his head back and forth, peering intently into the mirror that the ASN makeup woman held up in front of him, and brought his hand out from under the barber's cloth to point at a spot on the curve of his forehead just below his expertly teased and blow-dried hairline.

"Still a little glare here, Kris," he said. Skip was one of those television personalities whose off-screen voice and manner were exactly the same as on screen: he was as full-throated, earnest, and "on" when talking about a shiny bald spot as he was about a sudden-death U.S. Open playoff. The effect of this unceasing peppiness, interestingly enough, was of a man who was long on pizzazz but perhaps a little short on gray matter.

The thin, bespectacled woman patted on some more pancake makeup.

"Ah, nice," Skip said with warm admiration.

The Green Room had turned out to be a cramped corner of ASN's equipment tent fitted out with a folding chair and a tiny table, where Kristin Mellon, production assistant and makeup woman, administered cosmetics and other improvements, but only to those who merited them, such as anchors and visiting celebrities.

Skip, who had listened to Lee's story while issuing an occasional touch-up instruction to Kristin, now undid the cloth from around his neck and unfolded himself from the chair. He was six-feet-three and Robert Redford—handsome, a onetime third-string quarterback with the Miami Dolphins, who had more lately created a place for himself as a second-string color announcer with ASN; a career advancement, if you looked at it the right way.

"I tell you what, Lee," he said sonorously. "I've just had a great idea. Why don't you come on up into the booth for the final hour of the show? By then Torresdahl will be so far in the lead there won't be that much interesting happening out on the course and we can do kind of a tournament-from-hell wrap-up for the day. You know, tragedy on the links and all that. Now . . ." His white, healthy teeth flashed. "How does that sound to you?"

Not very appealing, but Lee would gladly take it. "You won't need me then until four o'clock?"

Skip laughed. "Look, I know what I'd do if I were you. I'd lay low. Carry around a manila envelope so if anybody sees you it looks like you're working. Think of it as a paid vacation. ASN can afford it."

But Lee, who had gotten just the answer she'd wanted, had something else in mind. "That sounds like good advice," she said, smiling, "but actually there is one thing I think I could do. Boyd was going to do a short feature for tomorrow about how the people here organized the tournament. He was supposed to be talking to them this morning, just preliminary interviews. Maybe I could get started on that in case someone wants to follow through?"

The idea had occurred to her on her walk from the trailer. Working on Boyd's project, she would have license to ask the Cottonwood board all kinds of questions about relations with ASN and the WPGL, about relationships within the board, about Ted, about almost anything she wanted. Although Peg herself was on the board, there was a lot that her friend didn't know. Peg had been a member only eight months and a Cottonwood Creek resident less than two years.

Before that, she and her husband, a research physicist at the National Laboratory in Los Alamos, had lived in Santa Fe, midway between their two places of work. But after Ric had twice bounced his car off the guard rails on Highway 502 because he was doing quantum optics equations in his head instead of paying attention to the narrow mountain road while on the long commute home, she had put her foot down. They had moved to Cottonwood Creek, which gave Ric an easy, level, seven-minute commute. As a result, Peg now had a two-hour drive to the management-consulting firm she'd founded in Albuquerque, but she did most of her work at her computer at home and spent only two days a week at the office. Besides, as even Ric freely admitted, Peg was a lot less likely than he was to do any woolgathering on the road. Or anywhere else.

"That's a terrific idea," Skip said, touching up a last stray tendril of hair with the help of the mirror and a moistened forefinger. He was obviously delighted to be off the hook as far as she was concerned. "You get right on it, honey. I'm sure it'll be real interesting."

"I'm sure it will, Skip," Lee said.

And with any luck, it might even lead somewhere.

* * *

As she came out of the tent Lee ran into Peg, who told her that Myrna Guthrie had gratefully invited them to call on her at 2:30 P.M. Would that suit Lee? Could she manage to get away from work for half an hour or so? Because if not, seeing the widow anytime soon would be a problem; Myrna was tied up for the rest of the afternoon and evening.

It suited Lee perfectly, leaving her well over an hour to try and locate the three other board members and see what could be gotten out of them. She found Frank Ayala first, making up for his interrupted ASN breakfast by wolfing down an open-faced barbecued beef sandwich in the members' dining room.

"All right if I join you?"

"I don't know, are you a member?" he growled at her, barely looking up from his plate. "Never mind, that's a joke."

I'm sure glad you told me, she thought.

Frank waved her into a chair and went on eating, cutting off a section of bread piled with ribbon-thin meat, stabbing angrily at it with his fork and more or less flipping it into his mouth. "Hell of a day."

He had managed to intimidate her from the moment she'd met him at Peg's party the night before. A brusque, self-confident, self-important sort of man, he hadn't taken long to make it clear that the 1990s weren't to his liking, particularly where women were concerned. Lee would have been willing to bet that he'd have been happier if they were still content to be seen and not heard. Or possibly not even seen.

"Mr. Ayala, they've asked me to follow up on Boyd's project—"

"Do you want something to eat? Some coffee?" He had

cleaned his plate, poured himself a cup of coffee from the pitcher on the table, and was now attacking a basket of *sopaipillas*, the puffy, deep-fried, sugared pastry that New Mexicans drenched with honey and seemed to consume with every meal.

She shook her head. Ayala had a stronger stomach than she did; they had both watched Boyd die less than three hours ago.

While he went on eating, she explained what she was doing, then listened with as much interest as she could feign while he told her in curt, impatient sentences about some of the delays, setbacks, and difficulties they had encountered in two years of planning. Ayala himself didn't seem very interested.

"I suppose," she said, doing a little fishing when he showed signs of getting restless, "that the whole thing must have been a pretty stressful experience."

"If you can't take the heat, you shouldn't be in the kitchen," he said, drizzling more honey from a squeeze bottle onto a *sopaipilla*. "We lost one of our board members because his ulcer started acting up. That's when Peg Fiske came on board."

"Yes, I know."

"Of course, who can blame him? Working with Guthrie was enough to give anybody ulcers."

"Oh, really?" she asked innocently. "Was Mr. Guthrie hard to get along with?"

An hour from now, once Ruben Torres had held his press conference, she wouldn't dare ask a question like that; after all, an edgy killer was running around loose and for all she knew she was sitting across the table from him right now. She was hardly eager to give Ayala or anyone else the impression that she was going around prying into Ted Guthrie's murder. But until Ruben made his announcement, there *was* no murder as far as anyone knew, so for the next hour at any rate, there was no undue risk in being nosy. She hoped.

Ayala appraised her over the rim of his cup. "You might say that," he said.

"Really? In what way?" She was working so hard at being naive that it took an effort not to bat her eyes. Not that it would make much of an impression on Ayala anyway.

He studied her a moment longer. "This is off the record. If you think I'm going to go on television and—"

"No, whatever you say."

"All right, he was overbearing, he was crude, he was stupid, he was ruthless, he was the most self-centered man I ever met, he was high-handed, he was a bully . . ." He gave it some more thought but was unable to improve on his list. "I know I've missed a few things, but that gives you a general idea."

Except for the parts about being stupid and crude, Lee suspected that Frank might get much the same rundown from those who worked with him. And she wasn't so sure about the "crude."

"And yet he managed to spearhead this tournament and actually bring it off."

"Or did the rest of us bring it off in spite of him?" Frank replied, then raised his hands to ward off more questions. "Please, don't get me started on Ted Guthrie. Not that I really minded him that much when it came down to it. It takes all kinds. Nice talking to you, I have to be going." He scrawled his name on the bill without bothering to examine it. "If you're interested, you ought to ask the others about him."

"I will if I can find them." Then, to be on the safe side: "I'm interested in every aspect of tournament planning."

"Well, I can tell you where Vernon Beal is," he said, getting up. He pointed over her shoulder, and when she turned she could see Vernon in the lobby, talking with considerable animation to another man of his own age who was dressed in old-fashioned plaid golf knickers. From Vernon's gestures, and from the other man's reactions—pursed lips, a slow, steady shake of the head—she guessed Vernon was describing what had happened to Boyd that morning. In faithful detail.

"Thanks, Mr. Ayala," she said, standing too. "I'll see if I can catch him."

He grunted. "Not that you're likely to get an objective answer out of him as far as Ted is concerned. Their relationship wasn't exactly sweetness and light."

"Yes, I heard that they were involved in some pretty hotly contested elections for board president."

Frank laughed. "I wouldn't call them 'contests.' Ted mopped up the floor with him. But that's only part of it." He turned serious, stopping as they left the restaurant. "I don't know . . . the way Vernon hated him, it ran deeper than that," he said, watching the older man, who still stood talking and gesturing about thirty feet away. "I'm no Sigmund Freud, but if you ask me . . ."

His finger went to his temple and described a few small circles.

". . . it was damn near pathological."

*   *   *

Her interview with Vernon was much briefer. "Not now, young woman," he interrupted as she went rather smoothly into her patter about the television feature. He had spotted another old crony who had just entered the lobby, and he was clearly itching to get to him before anyone else did and render his eyewitness description all over again. He nodded inattentively at Lee and began to move off.

"But they want to shoot the actual feature tomorrow," she said. "If we don't get the preliminary interviews done today, it's all off." Just when, she wondered a little uneasily, had she turned into such a glib liar?

But even the prospect of missing his chance to star on national television barely managed to compete with the pleasure of being the first among his friends with an insider's account of the sensational news.

"Well, perhaps I could give you a minute or two," he said grudgingly, regretfully watching his friend get snapped up by someone who hadn't even been in the ASN tent at the time. Still, his eye kept wandering over the room, searching out other likely quarry, and Lee had a hard time keeping his attention.

When she finally got the conversation around to Ted Guthrie as casually as she could, Vernon responded with a rambling litany of Ted's failures not too different from Frank's: Ted was wrong-headed, self-centered, smart-alecky, vulgar, devious, conniving. Not that Vernon himself had ever had any problem getting along with him, of course. No, ma'am, Vernon was a firm believer in live and let live.

More or less in passing, however, he did let drop the interesting fact that he wouldn't be surprised if Harry Harrelson had been feeling particularly aggrieved toward Ted lately. After all, the course redesign would change the view from Harry's living room windows from a striking panorama of rolling high desert to a not-so-striking panorama of double-tiered weekend condos seen from the rear.

That was about as much as she could get out of Vernon, and her subsequent meeting with Harry, held over an amicable pitcher of iced tea on the patio of his home not very many yards behind the fourth green ("Every time some hacker chooses a five-iron when he should have picked a seven, I wind up having to replace the dining room window. I keep a supply in the garage, precut."), was little more informative. But even Harry, the only one among them who had a few generous words for their deceased board president, couldn't help pointing out that it had always been his opinion that Frank's transparent dislike for Ted stemmed less from an instinctive aversion than from Ted's having steered several of his pals' lucrative deals away from Frank's investment-banking firm and into the clutches of Frank's chief rival.

What they told her, in other words (aside from more details than she had ever wanted to know about the nuts and bolts of setting up a golf tournament), was pretty much what she had already learned from Peg: that Ted Guthrie was a difficult and unlikable man who had managed in his relatively short stay at Cottonwood to make enemies at every turn; people who were undistressed, to say the least, at having him out of the picture.

But would one civilized man kill another over a spoiled view, a community election, a loss of some business? She didn't think so. And even if he would, where did Boyd come into it? Why kill him? No, if the two murders were connected, the reason for them lay in some linkage, some relationship, between the two men—not in the internal squabblings of an affluent country club.

There was, however, one undeniably useful thing she found out, and it was Harry she heard it from. The X ray she had taken the previous day showed no damage worse than the lateral epicondylitis he had already diagnosed. And after an on-the-spot reexamination of her arm at the patio table, he told her with every sign of pleasure that if she took care of herself, with any luck at all she would be back on the tour in a month.

Joy of joys, there was life after Mike Bulger.

Chapter 20

Even by Cottonwood Creek standards, the Guthries' house was imposing. An irregular, two-story, buff-colored, Pueblo-style building of knobbly, undulating adobe, with softly rounded edges, and with roof beams—*vigas*, they called them here—that stuck out through the walls, it stood in a handsome Southwestern garden of ocotillo, prickly pear, cottonwood, and juniper set among desert rocks and broad flagstone paths.

There were even fake Pueblo-style ladders that stood on the flat, lower-floor roof surfaces, leaning against the walls of the upper story. All in all, it seemed to Lee the kind of place you'd expect to see a Hopi Indian come out of. A well-to-do Hopi Indian, of course.

With Peg, she stood at the entrance to the property, an artfully weathered wooden gate in a picturesque fence of rough-cut pinyon poles.

"Well," said Peg, about to reach for the latch, "here we go."

"Is there some kind of regulation here that all houses have to be the same color?" Lee asked, looking up at the impressive structure. She had yet to see a white house in Cottonwood Creek, or a yellow one, or a green one, or a gray one, so the question was reasonable. Still, she knew that she was merely making conversation, trying to put off the moment when they met Myrna Guthrie. Facing recently bereaved widows was something she had little experience with—*no* experience, actually—and she was now having second thoughts about coming along with Peg.

"Certainly not," Peg told her. "We operate under the well-known Santa Fe–style building code here. It's extremely permissive. Forty-seven different varieties of brown are allowed."

Lee smiled. "That's like what we say about the colors you run into around Portland: you can see every shade found on the underside of a mushroom."

Peg began to laugh, then frowned. "I don't get it."

Lee shrugged. "You'd have to be born there." She sighed. "I suppose we ought to go in."

Peg looked sharply at her. "What's the matter?"

"Oh . . . nothing. I just feel funny about it. As if I'm intruding."

"Nonsense, she'll appreciate it. Myrna's one of these mousy, ineffectual little women. She's always been in Ted's shadow, you know, and without him she must be devastated. She's going to need all the support she can get. Besides, she asked to meet you. Didn't I tell you that?"

"No," Lee said, surprised. "Why would she want to meet me?"

Peg turned to give her a puzzled look as they went through the gate and stepped onto the flagstones. "Because you did your darndest to save her husband's life, or did you forget?"

"No, of course I didn't forget."

But she had. Or not forgotten, exactly, so much as not made the connection. So many things had piled one upon the other in the last twenty-four hours—Boyd's death, Graham's surprise arrival, being forced to quit the tournament, having the ASN job tossed into her lap—that her harrowing, fruitless effort to revive Ted Guthrie had dropped into a sort of long-ago, not-quite-real limbo. The gentle anesthesia of memory, she'd heard someone call it; the same mechanism that muted and softened one's recollection of a painful visit to dentist or surgeon.

Would Boyd's death be no more than a blurred memory tomorrow? No, she thought determinedly, it would not. She didn't intend to let it become one.

Myrna Guthrie was cut from much the same pattern as Mrs. Potter, the woman in whose house Lee had sat out the lightning storm: a few years younger, but with the same tiny hands and feet, the same porcelain-doll complexion of rose and white (not a complexion suited to the New Mexico sun), the same fussy, twittery, motherly manner. Maybe it was the way you were expected to be if you lived in Cottonwood Creek long enough. If so, they were going to have to make some serious adjustments for Peg.

She stepped out to greet them on the front step, a lace-trimmed handkerchief tucked under the wristband of her watch. Peg held out her arms, but Mrs. Guthrie shrank timidly back, as if afraid that a show of affection, however small, might break down her frail defenses against grief, and offered a rouged, powdered cheek instead. Then she held out her hand to Lee.

"Thank you so much for coming."

"I'm so very sorry about your husband," Lee said.

"Thank you, my dear." She squeezed Lee's hand and smiled bravely at her. "I want you to know how much we all appreciate what you tried to do. I know how much it cost you."

"Anybody else would have done the same," Lee mumbled and dropped her eyes in self-reproach when that small, nagging inner voice raised its pointless, mean-spirited complaint once more: Why couldn't it have *been* anybody else? Anybody but me?

The inside of the house took her by surprise. Where there should have been earth-toned walls, exposed beams, a beehive-shaped fireplace, and Navajo rugs, there was instead a living room out of an English country cottage: cheerful, floral-print curtains, wainscoted green walls, brass lamps, hunting and golfing prints, and overstuffed Victorian armchairs. The Guthries, it was clear, hadn't let the accident of living in the heart of New Mexico interfere with their tastes for Olde England. Lee's parents were much the same; if they ever got enough money together to build their dream home, which wasn't getting any more likely with time, it would be done up in a gorgeous, sunny, Spanish Colonial style. And sit on a misty, forested bluff overlooking the Columbia River gorge in the Pacific Northwest.

Mrs. Guthrie's grandniece Megan, a sulky twenty-year-old in halter and workout shorts, went to the kitchen to bring tea and coffee while the others gathered around the low, brassbound butler's table in the living room.

"Is there anything we can do?" Peg asked. "Anything you need?"

"No, dear, everyone's been so sweet. And Megan is an angel." She lowered herself with a quiet, widowlike smile into an armchair decorated with ducks on the wing and smoothed her skirt with a delicate, beringed hand. "And I have everything I could want right here."

Some nuance in the way she said it, or perhaps the discreet, veiled glance at the possessions around her made Lee sit up and wonder if she—and Peg—had misread the older woman. Myrna Guthrie might be newly and suddenly bereaved, but she was by no means withering away with sorrow. That brief, self-complacent glance had said it as clearly as words: This lovely house is all mine now; mine to use, and order, and arrange as I wish, when I wish, without permission, or consultation, or argument. Or having anybody else underfoot.

Evidently widowhood had its compensations.

Megan came back with coffee for Peg and Mrs. Guthrie, iced tea for Lee, and a plate of sugar cookies.

"Megan, dear," Mrs. Guthrie said, smiling, "I believe I did say the coffee cake."

"No, Aunt Myrna, you said the cookies. I remember, because—"

"No, dear, but let's not argue about it. Let's just have the coffee cake, shall we?" Mrs. Guthrie's smile was slightly strained.

Megan stood her ground. "I distinctly—"

"Oh, this is fine," Lee said. "It all looks delicious."

Lee saw Mrs. Guthrie mouth three silent syllables at Megan through a smile that by now might have been nailed on her face: *Cof . . . fee . . . cake.* Megan sighed theatrically and went back to the kitchen.

Well, well, Lee thought with interest, if Mrs. Guthrie was a mousy, ineffectual little woman, then Lee was the Queen of Prussia.

"Will you hold a service?" Peg asked gently. "I'd like to pay my respects. I know a lot of people would."

A frown of annoyance creased Mrs. Guthrie's papery brow. "I can't tell you what a bother that's been, Peg. Mr. Ivey at the funeral home says he needs three days to arrange things, but the police told me they're not sure when they can release Ted's corpse to me, so how can we plan? Oh, it's *very* irritating."

Again Lee's estimate of the widow's reserves rose. If she'd been in Mrs. Guthrie's place, would she have been able to refer to her longtime husband's "corpse" quite as nonchalantly as that? Even if he had tended to get underfoot sometimes?

"They're holding his . . . his body then?" she asked. "Did they say why?"

"Oh, it's just a matter of routine, I'm sure. Still, it's awfully annoying. People expect me to send out cards, you know."

Megan came back with the coffee cake and sullenly took her leave.

Mrs. Guthrie sliced the cake and handed it around. "Now," she said with an unseemly sparkle in her eye, "is it true that that nice Mr. Marriner really dropped dead this morning too?"

Yes, they told her, it had happened at breakfast in the ASN mess tent.

"A heart attack, I imagine. He was such a hard worker."

They didn't correct her.

"*Isn't* that something," she said, swallowing a pea-sized morsel of cake. "Here he and Ted were going to make all those wonderful changes at ASN next year, and now they're both gone. My, you just never know, do you?"

Lee and Peg glanced guardedly at each other. Had they stumbled on something already? A link between Ted Guthrie and Boyd?

"They were working on something together?" Peg asked.

"Well, in a way. You know Ted was a major stockholder in ASN, or rather in Meta Communications, their parent company, and a member of their board of directors—"

"Ted was on the board?" Peg said. "I had no idea."

"Oh, yes. And he'd been very impressed with Mr. Marriner's abilities, very impressed indeed. So much so that he got them to create an entirely new position for him, the vice—"

"Vice-president for golf," Lee cut in. "He was going to be promoted next fall. He told me."

Peg turned a baleful scowl on her. Lee shrugged apologetically. How was she supposed to have known it might be important?

"Yes," Mrs. Guthrie agreed sadly. She shook her head and clucked. "Such a young man, not even sixty. And so gentlemanly. Ted got along with him right from the start; not like some I might mention."

"At ASN?" Lee said keenly. "There were people your husband didn't get along with?" She winced. If she really intended to go around asking people leading questions, she was going to have to learn to be a little less obvious about it.

But Mrs. Guthrie didn't seem to see anything odd about the question. "Mr. Cochrane, for one," she said promptly.

"Skip Cochrane? The announcer?"

"Yes. Ted never did care for him. Of course," she added with a secret little V-shaped smile, "Between us girls, Ted wasn't always so easy to get along with himself."

"Oh, I wouldn't say that at all, Myrna," Peg said tactfully, if not quite truthfully. "He had a lot of strengths."

"What was the problem between them?" Lee asked as carelessly as she could. She broke off a piece of cake with her fork to show her indifference to the answer.

Mrs. Guthrie gave this some thought. "Well, you know, I really couldn't say, dear," she said, as if surprised to find that this was so. "I believe it was something or other to do with one of Ted's courses. Ted explained it all to me, but I've forgotten. I never did have a head for that sort of thing.

"But I know I don't like that young man one bit," she concluded loyally, then glanced up at the antique pendulum clock on the opposite wall. "Oh, my, I hope you won't think me terribly rude if I tell you I have a three-thirty appointment in Santa Fe—" She smiled at Peg. "—and you know how upset Mr. Fabrizio can get when you're late."

Chapter 21

"Who's Mr. Fabrizio?" Lee asked Peg as they drove back to the clubhouse over the gracefully curving streets of Cottonwood Creek. "Hairdresser," Peg answered, one elbow out the window, the other hand on the wheel of her white BMW. "Santa Fe's toniest."

Lee let a few thoughtful moments go by without saying anything before she spoke again. "I don't know that 'devastated' is exactly the word I'd pick for Mrs. Guthrie."

Peg threw back her head and laughed. "Let me tell you, there are depths there I never knew about." Then, more seriously: "I've been to the house a few times before. Ted had a favorite chair in the living room, one of those humongous, awful, adjustable ones with a big lever, you know?"

"I didn't see it."

"That's because it wasn't there. Neither were his ashtrays—Ted used to smoke an occasional cigar. Which Myrna couldn't stand."

"You're saying she didn't waste much time getting rid of any reminders of him."

"All of one day, to be exact, if that."

Lee looked at her. "Peg, you don't seriously think—"

"No, I don't. If every widow who blossomed when her husband cashed in his chips was charged with murder, there wouldn't be very many widows walking around loose. Anyway, if she could stand living with him for thirty years without doing him in, why bother now?"

Lee felt a guilty qualm to find herself laughing about murder, but maybe it was a good thing. Maybe she was distancing herself from it. From them.

"I agree with you," she said. "Besides, we're talking about two murders, and Myrna had no reason—no reason we know of—for wanting Boyd dead. And even if she did, she had no way of getting into the mess tent. You need a pass."

"But do you really? It's not as if somebody stands at the entrance checking everybody's card. If you wanted to bluff it out you could probably sneak in."

"Yes, but if you were trying to murder somebody, would you take that kind of chance on calling attention to yourself? Or even maybe getting kicked out before you could do it? I think you'd find some other way to do it."

Peg nodded thoughtfully. "Okay, that's a good point, but let's turn this around a little bit—not just on Myrna's account, but to think it through. We've been assuming that the food was poisoned *in* the tent. How do we know it wasn't already poisoned when it arrived?"

"Where would it have been done? In the Casa Rosita? In the delivery truck? The gatehouse? While Lou was carrying it to the tent? As far as I can see, those are the only other possibilities, and none of them seem very likely."

"No," Peg admitted after a moment, "they don't. All right, then, let's assume that whoever did it has a pass to the ASN mess tent. Next question: who has passes? Answer: the ASN personnel—Skip Cochrane, Mike Bulger, Mary Ann Cooper, and everybody else who's working for them. Fifty people, probably."

"A lot more than that, because you have to count people like Lou and me."

"Even so, at least we know the killer works for ASN in some capacity. Who else would have a pass?"

"You, for one."

"Me! I don't—oh, that's right, I do. Boyd gave me one to get in this morning."

"You, and Vernon, and Frank, and Harry, and anybody else Boyd felt like giving one to. Or anyone Mike or any of the other execs felt like giving one to."

Peg made a growling noise. "Listen, if my ideas are all so lousy, let's hear one of yours."

Lee shook her head. "Don't I wish I had some."

For the remainder of the short drive to the clubhouse parking lot they settled back, each with her own reflections.

"Well, at least Myrna did tell us something that might turn out to be important," Lee said as Peg guided the car into its slot. "There *was* a connection between the two men. Boyd's promotion was arranged by Ted."

"Yes, and between them they were going to make some big changes. Does that suggest anything to you?"

Lee looked at her and nodded. "You bet it does: the possibility that somebody didn't like those changes and decided to make sure they didn't go into effect."

"Exactly," Peg said, with a feisty, familiar gleam in her eyes. "I'd say that's worth looking into, wouldn't you?"

"You bet I would!" Lee said. "We could—" She stopped and slowly shook her head. "Peg, it goes against my grain to say it, but I think we'd better tell Ruben and Graham what Myrna told us, and let them do the looking. I don't think they'd be too happy to find out we were doing any poking around on our own. Serious poking, I mean."

Peg peered at her, her head cocked. "That boyfriend of yours really has you cowed, doesn't he?"

Lee laughed. "Yes, as a matter of fact. But in this case

he's right. This is their job, they know what they're doing. And we're babes in the wood."

"Speak for yourself," Peg said. "I'm older than Graham is . . . drat." She shifted on the seat to face Lee more directly. "Now listen. There's hardly anything for them to go on yet. Ted was going to promote Boyd, big deal. We need more details than that, and I'm telling you we could get them easier and faster than they could. The minute we find something they can use, we'll pass it right on to them. Even Graham couldn't argue with that."

"Ho-ho, says you. Peg, don't you think I'd love us to be the ones that hand over this creep's head on a platter? But we're not talking about some kind of game here. Two people have been killed. It isn't something to play around with."

"So how come *you* were out there buttonholing the board members with that cockamamie TV interview story and asking them all kinds of questions about Ted?"

"It wasn't a cockamamie story . . . well, not exactly. Besides, Ruben hadn't held his press conference yet. Everybody thought Ted's death was an accident—"

"Everybody but the person who killed him."

"—but the word's out by now—it's already three-fifteen—and if we go around asking funny questions about him now, somebody's liable to notice. I say we tell the police what we know right now and let them decide what to do with it."

Peg sighed and gave in. "You sure know how to poop a party, I'll say that for you. All right, you win. If you want me to, I'll call Ruben's office when I get back and tell him what Myrna said. Heck, he probably knows all about it already anyway."

"I wouldn't be surprised."

Peg glanced at her watch. "Now, get going, you only have three-quarters of an hour before you're due up in the booth and I want to get home and make some popcorn and watch you on TV. I'll see you at the club party later. Oh, and bring Graham, of course."

"Thanks, I will," Lee said, getting out of the car. She closed the door and leaned back into the open window. "You probably ought to tell Ruben about Skip too."

"What about him?"

"Well, that he and Ted Guthrie apparently didn't get along. Ruben might want to—what's so funny?"

"Lee," Peg said through her bark of a laugh, "have you met anybody yet that *did* get along with Ted Guthrie?"

*   *   *

First things first. The moment she left Peg, Lee headed for the mirror in the women's lounge. She was about to make her debut as ASN's temporary, stopgap, third-string women's golf color commentator, and she wasn't about to get caught on national television again with her face looking like a bowl of oatmeal with eyes. For once in her life, if she'd had the time she would have treated herself to a session with the WPGL's version of Mr. Fabrizio—a contracted beautician aptly named Roxanne LaFleur, who moved from city to city with the tour, doing her best to make sun-dried, windburnt golfers look human again and sometimes even glamorous if the raw material was there. But you didn't get in to see Roxie on less than two days' notice, so Lee had to make do on her own.

Having applied coatings of lipstick, rouge, mascara, and eyeliner to the appropriate regions, Lee went to the sparsely populated snack bar's vending machine for a quick Coke. She popped the top of the can, and sat at one of the tables to do a little thinking. High on her list of things to think about was Skip Cochrane. Sure, Peg was right about its hardly being big news that Skip or anyone else hadn't gotten along with Ted, but Skip had something that none of Ted's Cottonwood Creek enemies had: an association with Ted

157

and Boyd. Was it possible that he was in some kind of hot water with Boyd as well as Ted? Could it be that Skip had wanted the promotion that Ted had arranged for Boyd? Could it . . .

She swallowed some Coke from the can and sighed. She was just guessing. It could be a lot of things, or none of them. The question that counted was: what was the problem between Ted and Skip? And with Ted unable to speak for himself and Skip hardly likely to be forthcoming, finding out wasn't going to be easy.

She would talk to Graham about it, of course, but it would be nice if she could do a little more digging first and give him something more solid to go on. On the other hand, she'd really meant what she'd said to Peg about keeping their noses out of things. Still, if you thought about it, that kind of warning applied more to Peg than it did to her. Could anybody deny that Peg tended to be rather, well, blunt at times—like a bull in a china shop, if you wanted to be brutally frank—while Lee herself could be just a little more subtle, a little less obviously outspoken?

A little more disingenuous. If you wanted to be brutally frank.

But was she disingenuous enough to get anything out of Skip that he was determined to keep hidden? Even allowing for his less-than-giant intellect, she didn't think so. So who else might know something about it? Mary Ann Cooper, his co-announcer? Mike Bulger . . . ?

Her answer walked in in the form of the woman who knew everything about everything—Bonnie Harlow, who headed for the coffee carafe like a thirsty cowhand heading for the bar on a Saturday night in Dodge City. She filled a twelve-ounce Styrofoam cup, carried it brimming to Lee's table, and flopped down talking to herself.

"Unbelievable," she was murmuring. "Absolutely unbelievable. Lee, the gods are against us on this tournament.

That's the only possible explanation. It wasn't meant to be."

"What—"

Bonnie stopped her with a raised hand, downed a swig of steaming coffee, winced at the heat, and exhaled loudly. "I've just come from the most amazing press conference. They're saying it was murder."

"Murder? You mean Boyd?" Lee asked, deciding that ignorance was her wisest course. She hadn't been at the conference herself, after all, so how could she be expected to know otherwise?

Bonnie shook her head, taking small, quick sips of the hot coffee. "Ted. Guthrie. Can you believe it? Would somebody like to explain to me how a man that was struck by lightning can be a murder victim? What did the murderer do, exactly—willfully and maliciously tell him to go out in the rain?"

"Well, what did the police say?"

"Not much that made sense, love. Only that they had reasons for thinking it wasn't accidental. Does that make any sense to you?"

"No."

Bonnie wrinkled her long, slightly off-center nose. "Me neither. Ah, well, what do we know? The law, it works in mysterious ways." She gulped down the rest of the coffee, shook her head dejectedly, and went to get another twelve ounces. No wonder Bonnie was so never-endingly "on." Lee had heard of relaxed, mellow people being referred to as having been "born three drinks ahead." The bustling, effervescent Bonnie had been born three double-tall *caffè lattes* ahead.

By the same token, she was never depressed for long. "So tell me, how is it going with ASN?" she said as she sat down again. "Insane, aren't they? What do they have you doing?"

"Pretty much whatever I want, actually," Lee said with a smile, "but I'm off to the tower in just a few minutes. Skip asked me up to provide some color for the last hour."

"Oh, Skip," Bonnie said, lightening up. "Lucky you, you'll love working with him. What a sweetie, I adore him. All those *teeth*! Everyone loves working with Skip."

If ever there was a heaven-sent opportunity, this was it. "I'm glad to hear it," Lee said, then manufactured what she thought was a pretty good puzzled frown. "Although I thought I'd heard he didn't get along with Ted Guthrie."

Possibly she wasn't as subtle as she liked to think, because Bonnie put her cup down and stared at her. "Lee—you're not seriously suggesting that he had anything to do with—"

"—with what happened to Ted?" Lee exclaimed, looking astonished (she hoped) at the very notion. "Good gosh, no, of course not, Bonnie. It was just—well, I'd heard they'd had some kind of falling out, and I was just curious, that's all."

Weak as it was, it seemed to satisfy Bonnie. "Show me the man who hasn't had a falling out with Ted Guthrie," she said, "and I'll show you the next candidate for sainthood."

"So I keep hearing. But what did they fall out about anyway?" In for a dime, in for a dollar.

"Oh," Bonnie said, "some dumb thing. It wasn't a fall out, really. Skip made some remarks on the air about Bonnymead, and Ted got annoyed."

"Bonnymead?" The name had a familiar ring.

"One of Ted's more unfortunate redesigns, in North Carolina. Skip was covering a Seniors tournament last year, and he said that he'd liked the third hole more when the hazard in the dogleg was a plain old mud puddle, not an 'Oriental pond complete with island, bridge, pagoda, and working teahouse.' He also said the new fairway bunkers looked more like sandboxes than sand traps."

"I can see why Ted was annoyed."

Bonnie leaned forward with a suppressed gurgle of laughter. "But you know, the thing is, it was true. Besides, I don't think Skip was really trying to be snippety—let's face it, humor isn't the man's forte—he was just describing things the way he saw them."

"So what did Ted do about it?"

"Do?" She seemed surprised by the question. "What was there for him to do? He got miffed. What would *you* do? You know, if it'd been *Skip* who'd been found dead, you might have a case for wondering if Ted had had a hand in it, but what in the world would Skip have had against Ted?"

"Bonnie, honestly, I never—"

But Bonnie had caught a glimpse of the wall clock out of the corner of her eye and jumped up. "Oh lordy, how did it get to be ten to four? Why didn't you say something? I'm already five minutes late."

"I have to go too," Lee said, standing up alongside her. "Showtime. Gulp."

Bonnie reached over and squeezed her wrist. "Don't worry about it, you'll knock 'em dead, lamb," she said with a grin. "Break a leg."

Chapter 22

But the woman who knew everything didn't know quite everything, Lee mused as she hurried to the broadcast tower. For one thing, Bonnie was obviously unaware that Ted had been a major force in Meta Communications, ASN's parent company. And if he'd had the power to get Boyd promoted, wasn't it also possible that he'd had the power to get Skip demoted or even fired? That perhaps this was one of the "wonderful changes" he and Boyd had in mind at ASN?

And *that* would certainly provide Skip with something against Ted. And against Boyd too.

While she climbed up the ladder to the booth utterly ignored by the crowd at the eighteenth green (ah, the fickleness of fame) Susan Torresdahl sank her final putt to a burst of applause, closing out the day with a 69. Unless she came completely apart tomorrow, she was sure to end up with no worse than a second-place finish.

And the $46,546 that went along with it.

Best not to dwell on it.

*　*　*

The hour in the booth was easier than she'd anticipated. As it turned out, she was only on the air for the final twenty minutes, and even then the dreaded IFB headsets were worn by Skip and Mary Ann, not Lee, so there were no disembodied voices in her ear telling her to look at the camera, or not look at the camera, or counting off how many seconds she had left to finish her thought.

And Skip and Mary Ann, professionals that they were, carried the brunt of the conversation and made it seem just that: a conversation. There was some wistful talk about her own first-round 64 and her carom shot ("the shot heard 'round the world," Skip actually called it while Lee blushed). Then it was on to an uncomfortably ghoulish discussion of the "stark specter of tragedy" that had "haunted" the first High Desert Classic.

Lee tried to lighten it up with some less tragic disaster stories of her own, such as the time a golfer in the small African republic of Benin hit a drive that plinked a bird in midflight. The stunned fowl fluttered erratically into the open cockpit of a fighter jet about to take off from the nearby Benin Air Base, whereupon the startled pilot promptly rolled his plane into four Mirage jets parked in a row alongside the runway. All five planes—the whole Benin air force—were wrecked. And the name of Mathieu Boya was forever enshrined in golfing lore as the only golfer ever to put a country's entire air force out of action with one swing of his club.

At least it ended the broadcast on a light note, and both Skip and Mary Ann were laughing and relaxed when they pulled off their headsets.

"Done like a real pro," Mary Ann told her approvingly, using her thick, muscular legs to roll her chair back from the console and pulling a diet root beer from the cooler. "You're a natural, Lee. I think we could use you again tomorrow. What do you think, Skip?"

"Sure, you bet," Skip said. "You were great, kid. Let's do it again for sure."

Lee basked in the flattery. She *had* been pretty good, if she said so herself. "Well, shouldn't I check with Mike to see if he—"

Skip waved his hand. "Hell, I'll tell Mike; it'll be fine with him." He rose from his chair with a graceful, athletic movement and stretched luxuriously, accenting his trim waist and broad shoulders. Skip was one of those men who couldn't help preening with women anywhere in sight. "How did your project go today, the—whatever it was?"

"Cottonwood board preinterview sessions," she tossed off professionally, "to see if there was anything promising in the idea of a feature on how they went about setting up a tournament."

"That sounds like a real winner," Mary Ann said dryly, "almost as good as the one we had last week on the southern Canadian golf-club-throwing championships."

"Yeah, that was *good*!" Skip agreed. He waved and smiled to some delighted fans below. Bonnie was certainly right about those teeth. When Skip smiled, it was like someone opening up a piano lid.

"So how did it go?" Mary Ann asked Lee. "Are you going to recommend they shoot it?"

"I don't think so, Mary Ann. It's pretty dull stuff, and they spent most of their time talking about—" She glanced at Skip. "—Ted Guthrie."

Skip didn't flicker an eyelid, but Mary Ann laughed. "Skip's favorite person."

"Oh?" said Lee at her disingenuous best, "didn't you like him, Skip?"

"He was a schmuck," Skip said flatly, flicking off the power switches, "but in this business you see a lot of schmucks. I could take him or leave him."

"Preferably leave him," Mary Ann said, and then, at

Skip's irritated glance, added "Sorry." She didn't look particularly contrite.

"Let's get out of here," Skip said grumpily, "and let them come in and get ready for tomorrow."

At the bottom of the ladder he was still disgruntled. "If you want to talk to somebody who couldn't stand his guts," he muttered, absently reaching for an outthrust pen and program held by a starstruck, middle-aged woman, "you ought to go and talk to Mike Bulger."

* * *

Lee almost laughed as she watched Skip make his frequently interrupted way through the crowd. To hear him tell it, he didn't have a problem in the world with Ted. Neither—to hear them tell it—did Vernon Beal, Frank Ayala, or Harry Harrelson. Of course, just by the by, Frank had pointed out that Vernon's dislike of Ted was extraordinary, Vernon had suggested that Harry was extremely bitter toward Ted, and Harry had happened to mention the fact that the keenly competitive Frank Ayala had lost several lucrative business deals due to Ted's intervention. And now here was Skip telling her Mike was the man to talk to if she wanted to hear from someone who didn't like Ted.

Round and round it went, and what it amounted to was that everyone got along just fine with Ted Guthrie . . . but everyone *else* absolutely sizzled with hatred for him.

And as for Boyd, she'd yet to hear a word spoken against him.

Total of useful information for the day: not much. She hoped Ruben and Graham had been doing better than she was.

Chapter 23

They hadn't. It was a long-faced Graham who picked her up in the rented Escort and drove her back toward the Thrifty Owl Motel. There were only two pieces of progress he had to report. The first was that one of Ruben's men had turned up a sixty-foot length of uninsulated aluminum wire about five hundred yards from where Guthrie's body had been, in the deep desert brush just beyond the golf course's wire fence and within easy throwing distance of the cart path—very probably the "murder weapon," so to speak.

Inasmuch as a sixty-foot coil of wire was not something that could be conveniently concealed on one's person, they were proceeding on the assumption that the killer had hidden it in his or her golf cart and had given Guthrie a lift in the cart, possibly when the storm had come up. Under some pretext, the killer had probably stopped the cart, then (as the contusion behind the left ear indicated) had clubbed Guthrie unconscious; there were plenty of serviceable rocks lying around for the purpose. After that, it would have been an easy thing to loop the wire around his hand and fling the other end over the low-hung power line.

But it was impossible to get fingerprints from the wire, so at the moment it did little more than add confirmation to the theoretical framework they had built.

The second bit of progress was that, with Lou's help, they had fixed the time that Boyd's food had been in the near-deserted dining portion of the ASN tent available for adulteration: from 10:22 A.M., give or take a minute, until about 10:30, when the first groups of diners began to arrive. Eight minutes in all—plenty of time to poison the food and leave, but not nearly enough for the police to demand and check alibis. Not that they could possibly have gotten through all the alibis that needed checking anyway. Not in the one day that remained before people scattered to the four winds.

"Doesn't sound too good," Lee said sympathetically.

"No, it's been a lousy day. We spent a lot of it trying to piece together Boyd's activities over the last few days— who he talked to, where he went—because we thought it might be a quick way to some leads, but it hasn't gotten us anywhere. And we still have some big gaps. I don't know where he was Wednesday evening, or—"

"Have you tried his diary?"

His eyebrows lifted. "Diary?"

"Diary, journal, notebook. A little pad that fit in his pocket. He was always writing things down in it. Always leaving it behind too."

Graham wilted again. "Well, he must have left it behind somewhere, because he didn't have it on him and it hasn't turned up anywhere else. But thanks, we'll keep an eye out for it."

"Did you get a report from the lab?" she asked after a few moments, looking for anything that might give him some sense of headway.

"Yeah, they verified cause of death," he said without enthusiasm. "Nothing surprising."

It had been the chiles rellenos all right, or rather the quarter-teaspoonful of a deadly mixture of malathion and parathion that had been added to the fiery salsa that covered them.

"A quarter of a *teaspoon?*" Lee echoed. "And he died so—so quickly?"

Graham nodded. "Powerful stuff, especially in combination. Instant paralysis, cardiac arrhythmia, respiratory failure."

"But couldn't he taste it? Smell it?"

"Not with all that hot sauce."

"What kind of poisons are they, Graham? I mean, what are they used for?"

"They're pesticides. You can still get malathion in nurseries, but parathion's only used nowadays in commercial agriculture—for onions and artichokes and a few other crops—and you need a license to get it. It hasn't been generally available since the 1970s."

"So how could—"

"But apparently it lasts just about forever in the bottle. And there are still some places you're pretty likely to find it tucked away and forgotten on a storeroom shelf."

"Where? What places?"

"Guess," he said.

"How would I—Oh. Golf courses?"

"That's right. And in case you happen to be wondering: yes, there'd been a couple of dusty old bottles of the stuff in the greenskeeper's shed here at Cottonwood, not even locked up. Mel—the greenskeeper—says they were there when he took the job ten years ago, and he just never got around to getting rid of them. He was looking at them just a couple of days ago, thinking about it, he says." Graham shrugged. "Well, they're not there now."

"So at least you know where the poison came from."

"Apparently, but I don't see that it does us much good."

"But doesn't it? Look, Graham, did you know—before now, I mean—that there was such a thing as a greenskeeper's shed on a golf course?"

"Well, no, but if I'd given it some thought I suppose—"

"I think that qualifies as a no," Lee said. "But this person did. And not only that, he knew where to find this particular greenskeeper's shed. And not only *that*, he knew what malathion and parathion are and how to mix a fatal dose, so . . ."

She trailed off, not happy with where her thoughts were headed. For a few moments she stared out the car window. They were at the edge of the downtown area, turning from Diamond Drive, which had wound down in big, swinging curves from Cottonwood Creek, onto Trinity Drive, Los Alamos's main thoroughfare. On their right was a three-story building, rambling and desert-colored: the Medical Center, where she'd gone for her X rays the day before on Harry Harrelson's instructions.

"So?" Graham prompted.

"So whoever did this must have been someone who was pretty familiar with golf courses—with this golf course in particular—and with poisons too."

Like Harry Harrelson, she was thinking. Avid golfer. Doctor. Member of the country club board and thus likely to be a familiar and unremarkable figure in the greenskeeper's shed or anywhere else on the Cottonwood course. And conveniently outfitted with a temporary pass that would have gotten him into the ASN tent while Boyd's food sat unattended on the table.

She told this to Graham; reluctantly, because she didn't want it to be Harry. Frank Ayala, maybe, or Mike Bulger, or Skip, or a few others—those she could live with. But not sunny, twinkling, grandfatherly Harry. All the same, of course, it had to be told.

"Harrelson?" Graham exclaimed. "The doctor? He tried to save Boyd. He was the first one at his side."

"But did he really try to save him? How does anybody know?"

Graham shook his head and smiled. "I suppose that's true, but he also went out of his way to get the poisoned food and keep it safe until we got there. Do you really think he'd have done that if he were the one who'd poisoned it in the first place?"

"Sure he'd have done it, why not?" Lee replied heatedly, irked by that aggravating male superiority that crept even into Graham's voice from time to time, especially if they were talking about police matters. "The medical examiner was bound to find out Boyd was poisoned anyway, and there's nothing to connect Harry to the salsa any more than anyone else. So by making this big show about protecting the food, he makes himself *look* innocent. It makes plenty of sense to me, even if it doesn't to you."

Graham glanced at her. "Maybe it does at that," he said, never one to be aggravatingly superior for very long. He pulled the car to the side of the road. "We have a little time, and I've been cooped up all afternoon. Let's stretch our legs and talk about it some more."

They had stopped near a small park, the unpretentious site of one of the most prodigiously fearful achievements in human history. On this piece of land had stood the Manhattan Project's top secret Ice House, where the first atomic bomb was assembled in 1945. But the Ice House was long gone now. There was only a pleasant little patch of close-cropped lawns and benches surrounding a small pond with a modest fountain in the middle: Ashley Pond Park, a place for downtown shop clerks to stroll and eat their brown-bag lunches. Lee and Graham strolled along the path that circled the pond, stepping out of their way for two children absorbed in sailing a miniature, radio-controlled sailboat. Graham walked with his head down, his hands jammed into the back pockets of his jeans.

"What reason would Harrelson have to kill Boyd Marriner?" he asked.

"I don't know." Lee hesitated. "But I know why he might have wanted to kill Ted Guthrie."

She expected him to stop and stare at her, but he just kept walking. "All right, let's hear it."

"Ted's redesign for Cottonwood Creek was going to change his view from miles of desert to miles of condominium backyards."

Graham glanced wryly at her. "We police types prefer our motives a little more basic than that: greed, jealousy, revenge, you know? Spoiling a view doesn't rank too high on the list." But a few seconds later he surprised her by quietly adding: "Not that it hasn't been known to happen."

"I'm not saying it did happen, Graham. I'm just telling you something I happened to hear. I'm not even sure it's true."

"Uh-huh." Now he did stop, take her by the arm, and look directly into her eyes. "And how did you 'happen' to hear something like that, by the way?"

She returned his gaze, eyes wide open—maybe just a little too wide. "Um . . . how?"

"Yes, how? You're not going around doing your own little investigation, are you?" He was getting steelier by the second. "We've already talked about that, as I recall."

You talked about it, she thought, not me. But she didn't see much point in raising his blood pressure, so she shook her head meekly. "How could I, Graham? I've been working all day. You just hear these things, that's all."

"Lee, honest to God, if you—"

She started them walking again. "Graham, will you stop being so all-fired masterful for a while? It's more than a female can withstand. My hormones are quivering."

He looked at her and laughed. "Mine have been quivering for months. Which reminds me: what would you say to

171

checking out of the Thrifty Owl? My room's a lot nicer than yours and I could sure use some company. We could have four nights together." He smiled. His voice softened. "We've never had that much time, Lee. It'd be wonderful."

It'd be wonderful, all right, and yet something held her back, some feeling she couldn't name. It wasn't the need to keep her mind and energies focused on her golf, because she wasn't playing golf. And her TV job took little energy and less mind. It was the old fear, the fear that if she once let down her guard, if she once let him get too close, her resolve would melt away entirely, all the pain and effort she'd poured into her career gone for nought. He would steal her strength, her determination . . . No, that wasn't fair. Not steal.

But he would sure as heck distract it.

"I don't know," she said lightly, playing for time. "Isn't there some regulation against that kind of thing while you're on police business?"

"Who's on police business? I'm on vacation."

"Some vacation." She paused. "Let's talk about it after the party, all right?"

"Sure," he said mildly, but she thought she caught the hint of an inward sigh.

I'm not being coy, she wanted to shout at him, *I'm not playing hard to get. I'm just trying to keep my head screwed on straight.*

"How long do we need to stay at this party of yours anyway?" he asked. "We really do need to do some talking, Lee. It's time to straighten things out."

Her heart sank another notch. She didn't want to straighten things out, she didn't want to resolve matters. As far as she could see, there were only two ways they could go: she and Graham could get married, which she was certain he was going to suggest if she gave him the chance, or they could break up and go their own ways. Both alternatives

172

were too awful to face. Marrying would mean the end of any real career, and what would happen to her life then? On the other hand, without Graham what good was golf? Or life?

No, from her point of view it was better to leave things as they were, unsettled though they might be. But Graham had a point of view too, and it wasn't fair to him to keep putting him off.

"All we need to do is make an appearance," she said heavily. "Then we can go off somewhere and have this talk you're itching to have."

He surprised her with a peal of laughter. "Good God, you make it sound like a death warrant. Cheer up, will you? Trust me, I'm betting you're going to like what I have to say."

As always, his openness and optimism did lift her spirits. He was right about a lot of things; maybe he was right about this too.

"I sure hope so," she said and squeezed his hand. "Come on, let's get on to that party. There may actually be *food* there and I've hardly had anything since that apple fritter this morning."

Chapter 24

There was food, all right, and plenty of it, but the buffet tables weren't getting much business. Eight or ten people, Frank Ayala among them, had loaded their plates, but the rest of the two hundred or more in the room seemed happier to do their chatting with glasses, not plates, in their hands.

"We may have made a slight error of judgment in our gastronomic theme," Peg said glumly as she stood with Lee and Graham, looking down the long tables set up in the center of the club dining room.

Had they ever, Lee thought. The theme, unfortunately, was Mexican: mountains of blue-corn tortilla chips, salsas, cheese-stuffed jalapeño peppers, tacos, tamales, quesadillas, enchiladas . . . and chiles rellenos. The chips had had some takers, but the bowls of salsa beside them were untouched and pristine. The predominant sound in the room, other than the din of conversation, was the crackle and crunch of tortilla chips being eaten dry.

"It doesn't seem too awfully popular," Lee said gently.

"The thing is," said Peg, glumly swirling her margarita, "the menu was arranged weeks ago. It was too late to change it today. When I saw nobody was going to touch it I got up and made an announcement, but it didn't seem to help."

"What did you say?" Lee asked.

"I just talked some common sense. I told them they were being silly, that you could just as easily put poison in Swedish meatballs as chiles rellenos, so what difference did it make?"

"Gee, I wonder why it didn't help," Graham said.

"What a disaster," Peg muttered. "The club treasury laid out four thousand dollars for this."

Graham set down his bottle of Dos Equis and picked up a plate. "Not for me, it's not a disaster," he said. "I'm going to get myself some of those tacos, and maybe an enchilada or two. Lee?"

"Maybe a few chips," she said doubtfully. "My appetite seems to have disappeared for the moment."

"Not mine," Peg declared. "I'm getting my money's worth too." She made straight for the tray of chiles rellenos and dug resolutely in, while Lee halfheartedly plucked a cherry tomato from a bowl of raw vegetables.

"By the way," Peg said offhandedly to Graham, who was beside her at the tacos, "would you or Ruben have any interest in seeing a fairly complete dossier of Ted Guthrie's business affairs?"

He turned a surprised glance on her. "Sure, do you know where we can get one?"

"Yes, from me. His accountants in Albuquerque are faxing it to me tonight."

"Peg, that's privileged information," Graham exclaimed. "Even cops have a hard time getting data like that. Guthrie's bank is making Ruben jump through hoops and they're holding back anyway. How did you—"

"You should have come to me in the first place," Peg said serenely. "It all depends on who you know. Grubber & Crooke is an old client of mine, and Ed Grubber owes me a favor or two. Listen, why don't you come on over for breakfast tomorrow morning and I'll give it to you. You and Lee both come." She turned to Lee. "Unless you have to be at work at some grisly hour again, like seven-thirty?"

"Uh-uh," Lee said. "I think they're having trouble finding something for me to do."

"Good. How about eight o'clock then? So what are you looking at me like that for?"

The question was directed across the table solely at Lee; Graham had wandered off to the tray of enchiladas.

"You've been out poking around," Lee said accusingly. "I thought you weren't going to go around asking funny questions."

"I haven't been asking funny questions, I've just been sort of surfing on the Internet for gossip. I do it all the time. The E-Mail Tattletale, they call me, fastest rumormonger in the West."

"Look, Peg, I thought we agreed we wouldn't—"

"Tell me," Peg interrupted blandly, "was your interrogation of Bonnie productive?"

Lee blinked. "My—how—"

"I have my sources. And were you able to get anything valuable out of Skip? What about Mary Ann?"

"No, nothing," Lee said, laughing. "Look, I just want you to be careful, that's all."

"You too, Lee—"

"Did I hear somebody mention my name?" It was Mary Ann Cooper, a little flushed and somewhat unfortunately playing the vamp in red miniskirt and high heels that made her bunchy, muscular legs look more Olympian than ever.

"Did you or did you not promise to introduce me to Mr. Right tonight?" she asked Peg.

"You know, I've been rethinking that," Peg said. "Lavor would probably be a little old for you, Mary Ann, and he's really not everybody's idea of Prince Charming. In fact he's nobody's idea of Prince Charming. I'm not so sure—"

"How rich is he?"

"Very."

"Heck, sounds like Mr. Right to me," Mary Ann said, taking Peg's arm. C'mon, let's go find him."

Lee went to find Graham, but by now he had been collared by Skip Cochrane and some other ASN people and was busy fending off questions about the murders. While he extricated himself Lee picked up a piece of celery and a club soda and looked around the room. She waved to a couple of fellow golfers, said hi to Bonnie Harlow and to Mickey Duff, the WPGL trainer, and was momentarily puzzled when a vivacious, smartly turned-out, elderly woman caught her eye and waggled her fingers in greeting.

Myrna Guthrie, Lee thought in amazement, already out and about on the party circuit. Or maybe not so amazing, come to think of it. She took a closer look. Mr. Fabrizio had done a sterling job, all right. Myrna's gray hair, plain and housewifely that afternoon, was now elegantly swept back. And unless Lee was seeing things, it wasn't exactly gray anymore, but well on its way to an attractive ash blonde.

"Hey, you were terrific today!" Mike Bulger shouted in Lee's ear.

"Why, thank you," she said, surprised. Well, what do you know, Mike was actually capable of saying something nice.

"Look, Lee—"

And he even knew her name. Wonder on wonder.

"—I want to try you out on some on-course commentary tomorrow."

"I think Skip and Mary Ann wanted me in the booth—"

"Yeah, well, they'll just have to handle it themselves. I

got bigger and better things in mind for you." He stood directly in her path, his hands on his wide hips. "I want you on the wrap-up interviews at the eighteenth green, how's that?"

He grinned benevolently at her. Obviously, from his perspective he had just dropped a plum into her lap.

Not from Lee's, however. She broke into a light sweat simply remembering what a botch she'd made of Jane Silberberg's taped interview that morning. Five takes. Live TV would mean only one chance to get it right. "Mike, are you sure I'm ready for that?"

"Don't worry, I'll walk you through it personally over the IFB."

That was all she needed: a hysterical Mike Bulger (by wrap-up time tomorrow he'd be hysterical again) screaming directions into her ear while she tried to conduct a rational conversation in front of several million people. But she couldn't very well say no. Her shoulders drooped. "Well, if you think I can handle it—"

"Piece of cake. And that's not all. I want you to do some introductory commentary at F-17, about, you know, strategy. Hey, don't look so worried, we record it ahead of time. You can do it with one hand tied behind your back. Look, I'll have Petey fill you in on everything you—"

"F-17?" she repeated, frowning. Something flickered in her memory.

He was starting to show signs of impatience. "F-17, F-17. The camera station on the seventeenth fairway?"

"I . . ."

"You know, *camera*? C-A-M—"

"F-14!" she said abruptly.

Mike stared at her. "No, F-17. What's with you any—"

"Mike, excuse me, I'll talk to you later."

"What? Hey, but—"

"And thanks a lot, I really appreciate the opportunity," she called over her shoulder, hurrying back toward the buffet table and very nearly colliding with a slightly tipsy Vernon Beal, who ducked out of her way like a turtle popping back into its shell.

"Graham!"

By now he had managed to shed his circle of questioners. He looked up from his first, rather large bite of taco.

"The notebook," she said excitedly, "Boyd's notebook! I think I know where it is!"

"Ulg?" was the best he could manage with his mouth full, but he was definitely interested.

"I know he had it just before he went in to breakfast this morning because I *handed* it to him just before he went to clear up the problem at F-14. I just remembered. So if he didn't have it when he died he must have left it there. Maybe it's still there. What do you think?"

But as she spoke, Cottonwood Creek's resident country music band, Chuckwagon Billy and His Texas Has-beens, began the evening's entertainment with their finger-pluckin', foot-stompin' rendition of "Mammas, Don't Let Your Babies Grow Up to Be Cowboys," and Lee had to shout it all over again.

"It's possible," Graham shouted back. "What's F-14?"

Lee put down her club soda. "The camera tower on the fourteenth fairway. We can walk to it. I'll show you."

"You'll tell me," Graham said. "You're staying put."

Lee laughed. "Right. And how are you going to find the fourteenth fairway—in the dark, no less? I have the course practically memorized. I could get us there blindfolded."

"Lee—"

"Besides, it's a beautiful night out there. And it's *quiet*—no Chuckwagon Billy."

"Next up, folks," said Chuckwagon Billy into the microphone, "is that old favorite of yours and mine, 'Does Your Chewing Gum Lose Its Flavor on the Bedpost Overnight?' Here we go, boys, a-one, and-a-two, and—"

Graham grinned, took one more bite of taco, and grabbed her hand. "You talked me into it. Let's go."

Chapter 25

A walk of less than two hundred yards, half the length of the eighteenth fairway, took them into a world of silence and pearly darkness. The plangent strains of "Does Your Chewing Gum Lose Its Flavor on the Bedpost Overnight?" had mercifully died away, to be replaced by the overpowering hush of the desert at night. There was only an occasional croak from a contemplative-sounding frog; that and the faint hum of the blood in their ears. Otherwise, nothing, not even their footsteps since they had left the cart path to cut across fairway grass as soft as velvet.

Lee had forgotten the feel of the nighttime desert: the stillness, the sweetness of the air, the brisk but welcome chill, the hint of dew, fresh and fragrant. There was no moon, but the broad, shimmering belt of the Milky Way—now there was a sight you didn't get to see in Portland very often—gave more than enough light to see by. The flashlight Graham had borrowed from the club manager was in his pocket. Around them the enormous expanse of fairway was silvery, the junipers on the hillside like pewter sculptures, the jagged rim of the Jemez Mountains a deep black against the paler black of the sky. In the west a faint smudge of rose remained where the sun had gone down.

"Nice," Graham breathed, his first words since they'd left the clubhouse.

"Mm," she said, feeling tranquil and close to him. In a way, she wished things could simply go on like this, the two of them walking side by side in the cool starlight, with no impending "resolution" looming over them. Graham seemed to feel the same way, taking quiet pleasure in this rare solitary moment with her, his hankering for that fish-or-cut-bait discussion on hold for the time being, anyway.

Neither of them was in any hurry to get to the tower. They skirted the seventeenth green, walked along another shadowed cart path for a while, and angled across the four-teenth fairway, not talking, just breathing in the clean, spicy air. Once, as if by spoken agreement, they stopped for a kiss, chaste and gentle, with Graham's hands framing Lee's face, then walked slowly, mutely, on, hand in hand. It took them a blissful, timeless twenty minutes to reach the tower.

"You want me to go up in *that*?" he said, looking up at it. "I used to build better towers than that with my Lego set."

He had a point. Like the other camera towers, F-14 was a flimsy-looking framework of metal pipes with a railed wooden platform, more a scaffold than a floor, on top. This one, however, looked more rickety than most because of the extra height that had been added to it, putting the platform more than twenty feet off the ground. The structure was set alongside the cart path in the left rough, a narrow, unforgiving swath of low cactus, stony gullies, and up-tilted, jagged slabs of rock, about 250 yards from the four-teenth tee, providing a head-on view of the landing area for most of the drives.

Graham pushed on the pipes, then tugged at the metal

ladder bolted to one side. "Well, it's sturdier than it looks," he said doubtfully. "What the hell, it's in a good cause. You stay down here. I don't think you ought to try climbing with your arm the way it is. I'll only be a minute."

"Don't be ridiculous," Lee said, brushing by him and scrambling up. Tennis elbow or not, she was an old hand at ladders and heights. As a teenager she'd earned after-school money by signing on as a plasterer's helper at some of the construction sites her father had worked at, and she had put in plenty of time on similar scaffolding three and four stories off the ground.

Graham came up behind her. "A lot higher than it looks," he muttered uneasily as he stepped onto the platform. She got a certain nasty satisfaction from realizing that the always-confident, always-competent Graham Sheldon wasn't quite as comfortable around heights as she was.

The platform was roomier than it appeared from below, but still cramped, with a plastic-shrouded tripod-camera lurking sinisterly in one corner, two metal equipment trunks along the railings on the sides, and, beside the camera, a wheeled cabinet with two open shelves cluttered with manuals, paper, and electronic paraphernalia.

While Lee held the flashlight Graham knelt and began rummaging on the shelves. "What's it look like?"

"Red, I think," she said, "or maybe burgundy. Shirt-pocket-size. Kind of cheesy . . ."

"What do you know," he said and dug it out from under a pocket calculator. "Bingo."

It had taken no more than a minute to find. She focused the beam on it and leaned excitedly over his shoulder while he leafed through it, still on his knees.

"Hard to say how useful it's going to be," Graham said, but he sounded excited too. "Appointments, names, reminders to himself . . . a lot of abbreviations." He thumbed the pages more rapidly. "He doesn't seem to have dated his entries, unfortunately, so it's going to be hard to say when he wrote what, but still . . ."

W. nuts & ct. tstr, Lee read over his shoulder. "Wing nuts and circuit tester!" she exclaimed, jabbing a finger at it. "That's his list for the hardware store. He was talking about it yesterday!"

"So? Am I missing something?"

"He went to the store Thursday night," she explained. "Which means he must have written this down sometime Thursday—the first day of the tournament. So anything that comes after it had to have been written after the tournament started, after he got to Los Alamos. Doesn't that help you?"

Graham considered. "It might at that." He snapped the notebook closed, slipped it into his jacket and patted the pocket with satisfaction, then got to his feet. "Look, what do you say we get this over to Ruben right now, then go and find a good restaurant someplace all by ourselves?" he said, raising his voice over the rumble of heavy equipment that had started up nearby. "We could talk."

Oh, dear, it was back to fish-or-cut-bait time again. Automatically, she began to hedge, but then thought better of it. It wasn't fair to Graham to keep putting it off; not to herself either, really. As restful as it was, they couldn't remain forever in this starlit never-never-land. There were some practical, long-overdue decisions that had to be made, and lives to be gotten on with. But, Lord, how she hoped that it wasn't going to be the last dinner she ever had with him.

She squeezed his hand. "Good idea," she yelled back, trying to look as if she thought it was.

"Great, what kind of food?"

"Anything but Mexican," she shouted. Whatever the machinery was it was making its noisy way down the cart path in their direction. Funny that it should be out at night.

He laughed, said something she couldn't hear, and softly

touched the back of her neck with his hand. She pressed his wrist against her cheek and moved impulsively against him. "Graham, I love you so much."

His response was unexpected. "What the hell?" he said.

And suddenly, inexplicably, she was sprawled on the floor and seeing stars—the-inside-the-skull kind—her head having thumped painfully against one of the metal trunks. *An earthquake . . . ?* she wondered confusedly, feeling the platform sway beneath them.

Graham was on his back too. In fighting to keep his balance he had snatched at the wheeled cabinet, taking it down with him and scattering paper and electronic junk all around them. The noise from below was terrific: a roaring and grinding and screeching straight out of hell. Lee lay still, trying to hold on to the plywood platform with her fingertips, willing the dizziness away.

Graham scrambled to the edge on his hands and knees and clutched the railing. "Hey, down there!" he shouted furiously. "*Hey*—!" He turned back to Lee. "Grab something! Here it comes again!"

By now the wisps of fog had cleared from her mind. It wasn't an earthquake that had almost knocked them off the tower, it was a tractor, or bulldozer—or maybe an Ml tank, if the racket was any guide. Not an act of God but an act of man, and whoever it was was about to take another crack at them. She flung herself at one of the corner posts that held up the railing, alongside Graham. He quickly wrapped one arm tightly about her, holding on to the post for dear life with his other hand. Together they watched helplessly as the thing came clanking back at them. It was a bulldozer all right, flat gray in the starlight, with exhaust belching from the smokestack. With the driver hidden by the roof, the huge machine seemed full of a creepy malice of its own, like something out of a horror movie.

When it struck this time, she thought the tower was

going down for sure. Over it slowly tipped, and over, with the monstrous machine thrusting at it like a fighting bull lunging at a picador's horse. Behind them an equipment trunk slid across the plywood floor and into the railing, and the camera broke from its mounting, tipped over the railing, and crashed heavily on the rocks below. Lee and Graham were clinging to the post as if it were a tree limb sticking out of the side of a cliff when a pipe joint somewhere beneath them gave way, tilting the tower abruptly to the left. Somehow they hung on through it. By now Lee wasn't sure she could loosen her fingers if she wanted to.

The bulldozer grumbled and snorted as it shifted gears, backed off a few yards and came on once more at full throttle. This, Lee knew in her heart, was going to be it. She wanted desperately to say something to Graham, if only his name, but somehow she had gotten twisted away from him, her face now pressed against the rough wood of the floor. Her ears were filled with the dozer's noise, her nostrils with its exhaust. She clenched her jaws, shut her eyes, tensed . . .

The base of the tower caved in as if it were made of Popsicle sticks. The upper part tilted still farther to the left, momentarily hesitated as if struggling for balance, then finally gave in and tipped beyond the point of no return. Lee's stomach seemed to fall away. She heard herself yelp as it plummeted—nothing slow-motion about it this time—but partway down it hit something—a tree, a rock—that stopped its progress with a jolt that broke their holds on the post and catapulted them head-over-heels over the railing and into the night.

Earth and stars spun crazily. She couldn't tell which way was up, which down. Convulsively, she tried to protect her head with her arms. At the very last moment, instinct took over. Her eyes shut again. Every muscle cringed, flinching from the impact, the bone-shattering—

Splash.

Chapter 26

Splash? She found her legs and came up sputtering and coughing. And utterly bewildered. Draped in weeds and algae, she was standing in water up to her armpits and what felt like mud up to her ankles. Water! What had happened to the rocks, the—

Graham surged to his feet a few yards away, whalelike, spewing water from nose and mouth.

"Graham! Are you—"

"Lee! Are you—"

They stumbled into each other's arms. "I'm fine, I'm fine," they panted gratefully, over and over, laughing, their fingers gently stroking each other to make sure it was so. In the distance the sound of the bulldozer was fading away.

"Your arm?" Graham asked into her streaming hair.

"No worse, I don't think. Who cares, it's good to be alive." She laughed shakily. "I always heard the earth was supposed to move when you were in your lover's arms, but *that* was ridiculous."

Graham laughed too, a little shaky himself. "I'll tell you one thing: you're never going to hear me say that golf courses are the most boring places in the world again. Christ, they make my old beat in Oakland look like Sesame Street."

By the time they came apart, shivering in the cold, they understood what had happened. When the pipe joint had given way and the tower had tipped so sharply to the left, it had tilted away from the rocky patch into which it had been headed and toward the cart path behind it that ran between the fourteenth and sixteenth fairways. And right on the other side of the cart path was a four-foot-high earth berm. And right on the other side of the berm, Lee thought light-headedly, on the other side of the berm was the far end of the pond, the wonderful, splendid, reed-choked six-teenth-fairway pond that had been the bane of the players since the tournament had begun.

When the tower had struck the berm on the way down—it was still propped crookedly against it—the shock had tumbled them into all this lovely, smelly, slimy water. On Thursday, during that wondrous first round, she had cleared this pond when she'd needed to. And now, when she'd needed to even more, she had fallen plop into it, along with Graham.

By now it was well on its way to replacing the Pacific Ocean as her favorite body of water.

"I don't know what there is to giggle about," Graham said. "Somebody just tried to kill us."

"I know," she said and made a quavery effort to compose her face. "I will endeavor to be more . . . more decorous."

At that they fell laughing into each other's arms again, radiantly happy to be alive and in one piece. "Graham, Graham, Graham . . ." Lee said into his shoulder, gradually calming down. They squelched through the mud to emerge shivering and dripping on the shore thirty or forty feet from the collapsed tower, their shoes full of muck.

"My good shoes," Graham said sorrowfully. "Wouldn't you know it? My one decent sport coat."

"Fortunately," Lee said, still a little giddy, "I have scads of these gorgeous, fashionable outfits. Thanks to Kmart's August two-for-one sale." She pulled viscous threads of algae out of her hair. "Yuck. What do we do now?"

"Call the police, what else? We can do it from one of those houses. Then get into some dry clothes. Then get some hot food into us."

It sounded good to Lee, especially the last part. "We can call from there." She pointed at a well-lit house not far from the fourteenth tee. Unless she was mistaken, it was Mrs. Winfield Potter's house, where she had sat out the storm on Friday.

"Why there in particular?" Graham asked as they started for it, leaving slithery trails in the grass like a couple of slugs.

"Because we look—and smell—like the walking dead, and I don't want to scare anyone out of their wits. Mrs. Potter's used to me showing up on her doorstep looking like a drowned rat."

"What about me?"

"Are you kidding? She'll love you."

* * *

True to Lee's expectations, Mrs. Potter, clad in a buttoned-to-the-neck duster and old sheepskin slippers, but with every crimped blued hair in place, rose to the occasion. Unsurprisingly, it had taken her a moment to recognize the bedraggled, cold-hunched figure on her doorstep as Thursday's leading player, but once that was accomplished she had sprung efficiently into action, producing bath towels from the cupboard, hot buttered whiskeys from the microwave, and piping hot showers, discreetly but pointedly assigning them to different bathrooms.

Before they'd finished toweling off, dry clothing was waiting for them. For Lee there was a collarless, cream-colored pantsuit, considerably more expensive than her usual wear but three inches short in the arms and legs. Fortunately the waistband was elastic. In addition there was a pair of fluorescent green-and-blue jogging shoes, the only shoes that her feet would fit into.

Graham had fared less well. "Naturally, I don't have any men's things in the house," Mrs. Potter had said with a becoming blush. "Dr. Potter passed away some years ago, but Mr. Spalteholtz two doors down is a tall man like you, and I'm sure he'll have something."

But Mrs. Potter obviously had no eye for men's sizes, because the gray sweatsuit she returned with had been made for a seven-footer. Graham looked lost in it, like a kid trying to wear his father's clothes. Lee, hardly in a position to cast stones, had burst out laughing all the same when he came out with it on, the general sartorial effect not helped by the dangling, size-fifteen leather slippers that the giant Mr. Spalteholtz had also donated.

A few minutes later they had met Ruben and one of his officers at the tower, given them what information they could, and turned over the soaked but legible notebook. The bulldozer had already been found a few hundred yards down the path, alongside the eighth fairway, with the key still in the switch. It had been taken from the equipment yard not far from the clubhouse, and a call on Mr. Connors, the equipment manager, had established the fact that stealing it had presented no great problems. The yard was rarely locked, and it was customary to leave the keys to the equipment behind sun visors or under seat cushions overnight for easy retrieval in the morning.

"Well, why not?" Mr. Connors had demanded querulously when Officer Lewis had expressed mild surprise. "Who in his right mind would steal a bulldozer?"

Hungry and exhausted, Lee and Graham had driven to the Thrifty Owl, where the generally immobile Marie, ensconced as usual on her stool behind the counter, had opened her mouth and billowed halfway to her feet, bracelets jangling, when they strode in, Graham's slippers slapping the linoleum tile.

"Well, look at you two!" she cried, her tiny eyes glittering at what was clearly the most interesting sight to come through her lobby in a long time . "Howdja—"

Lee leveled a finger at her. "Don't . . . even . . . ask," she said warningly.

"I didn't say nothing," Marie said, holding up her hands but goggling avidly at them as they swept imperially by her and up the stairs, with Graham slap-slapping every step of the way. "You can tell me all about it later, hon," she called hopefully after them.

"We look like Mutt and Jeff," Graham grumbled on the way up. "I'm just not sure which one's Mutt and which one's Jeff."

Neither was Lee. They were both from well before her time, but this didn't seem like the moment to point it out to Graham.

"Now, listen," he said after she'd changed into a sweater and jeans and was briefly, hopelessly, trying to do something about her hair, "I don't want you staying here by yourself anymore. Right after dinner I want you to move out of here and over to the Los Alamos Inn with me."

Brush in hand, she turned to look at him. "Graham, I—"

"I'm not talking romance, I'm talking security," he said gruffly. "Somebody's just done their damndest to kill us."

"I—"

"I just don't want you being alone for the next few days, is that so hard to understand?"

"Graham—"

"And I don't want any debate, dammit. Is that clear?" He scowled just a bit self-consciously. "Well, say something."

She laughed, put down the brush, and came up to him to lay both hands on his shoulders. "I've been *trying* to say something. I'm all for it. I agree with you. I'll pack up right now, this minute, not after dinner."

"You *will?*" He was so surprised his voice broke. "You're not going to argue with me?"

She shook her head. "I think it's a wonderful idea. And," she added, "I'm not necessarily talking security."

He grinned at her, transparently relieved. "Want me to help you pack?"

"No, why don't you go down and check me out? I don't think I quite have the nerve to face Marie just yet."

"I will," he said and went to the door, then paused to face her with a sigh.

"The things I do for love."

Chapter 27

They drove to the Los Alamos Inn, where Graham changed to a chamois-cloth shirt and jeans and a pair of shoes that didn't flop, and Lee dropped off her things in his admittedly classier room (the lightbulbs all worked, the closet had a door, and the TV set wasn't bolted down). They spent the half hour this consumed hashing over the evening's traumatic turn of events from a dozen different angles, not getting much of anywhere beyond the obvious.

They concluded, for example, that Boyd's notebook had to contain something of vital importance, something critical enough to prompt the killer into his loony armored assault on the fourteenth-fairway tower. And that whoever it was must have been at the party and overheard them. How else would anyone have known where they were headed and why?

"In a way," Graham said, slipping into a windbreaker, "this was a lucky break—"

"If this was a lucky break," Lee said, "I hope I'm not around when you run into an *un*lucky one." She gathered the soft, rolled collar of her sweater around her throat. Despite the hot shower, the change of clothes, and the seventy-degree temperature in Graham's room, she was still chilled.

"I meant lucky from the police's point of view," Graham said. "When I finished up with Ruben this afternoon we had a thousand suspects—which is the same thing as saying we didn't have any. Now all of a sudden there are only a couple of hundred possibilities at the most. And it isn't going to be hard for the police to piece together exactly who was there."

"That's true. And maybe they can find out if anybody disappeared for a convenient half hour or so at about eight o'clock."

They closed the door behind them and headed for his car. "Well, that's a lot harder. Just because nobody remembers seeing Mr. or Ms. X for a while doesn't mean they weren't there. But you and I ought to be able to boil it down a little more by seeing if we can remember who might have been within earshot when we were talking."

That was harder than it might have been under ordinary circumstances, however, because Chuckwagon Billy and his boys had been belting out their advice on child-raising at the time, and she and Graham had been shouting loudly enough for "earshot" to extend halfway to the Arizona border. Nevertheless, they had put together a list of the people they remembered as having been reasonably close by: besides a few of the golf pros, there were Skip Cochrane, Mary Ann Cooper, and Mike Bulger of ASN, Bonnie Harlow and Mickey Duff of the WPGL, and Frank Ayala, Harry Harrelson, and Vernon Beal of the Cottonwood Creek board. Also some other country club members that Lee had met but couldn't name, and several ASN and WPGL staffers whose names she likewise didn't know.

By the time they had compiled this roster they had driven back across Los Alamos's lamp-lit, nearly deserted downtown to the Trinity Sights restaurant, which Peg had earlier assured them was the city's finest. They had both agreed that they more than deserved a good meal.

"As it turns out," Lee said as they parked in the lot, "I've been hearing some, um, interesting things about a lot of those people. I mean, I don't know how much of it is true, but . . . ."

Graham listened, head down, drumming on the steering wheel, while she told him about the alleged bad blood between Skip and Ted Guthrie over Skip's insufficiently respectful public remarks about the redesign of the Bonnymead course; about Vernon Beal's unconcealed hatred of Ted over the loss of the board presidency and who knew what else; about Frank Ayala's—

"No, whoever it was, it wasn't Vernon Beal," Graham said. "Wasn't he the garden-variety geezer, the one you sent off for the medics when you found Guthrie? Why would he run off and try to get help if he'd just electrocuted him?"

"If he already *knew* Ted was dead, of course he'd run for help. Why not? He'd look suspicious if he didn't."

"Well, *maybe*, but if I remember right, Beal's also the one who tried to talk the board and the WPGL into canceling play on account of the lightning. Does that make sense if he was planning to kill him the way he did?"

"It certainly does," Lee said, warming to her own idea. "Vernon knew perfectly well that they weren't going to cancel. He could easily have been arguing for show, so people would remember it later and write him off as a suspect. Which, may I point out, is exactly what you're doing."

"You," Graham said, "have been watching too many old *Columbo*s. Now what were you going to say about Frank Ayala?"

"Frank loathed Ted. Possibly on general principles, possibly because Ted steered some business to one of his competitors. And Harry Harrelson—"

"You already told me why Harrelson was insanely homicidal when it came to Guthrie," he said dryly. "The view from his living room window was spoiled."

"Look," Lee shot back, "just because you don't want to take anything I say seriously—"

"Dammit, I *do* take it seriously."

"Then why are you being so—"

He turned to face her directly. "I'm annoyed, is why. I wish *you* took it more seriously." He was as close to being angry with her as he'd ever been. "How the hell did you come by all this information? You've been snooping around, asking questions, thinking you're so clever, figuring that us poor, dumb coppers don't stand a chance of solving this on our own, that we need *you* to help us see which way is up. You and Peg. Well, let me give you some news: we don't."

"Have you finished?" She had drawn herself up while he spoke. "I have not been snooping around, as you put it," she said acidly. She was thoroughly put out with him, which was entirely his fault for being right on all counts. "I have been busy with my work for ASN. And when you are engaged in interviews and research with a wide variety of people, you, um, uh, happen to hear certain things."

"Yeah," he said sourly, "and where have I, um, uh, heard that before?" He shoved open the car door on his side. "Come on, we better get something to eat before they close the place up."

It took a crabby, silent elevator ride and most of a whiskey toddy apiece before they felt sufficiently sheepish to apologize to each other.

"That's the longest we've ever stayed mad at each other," Lee said, relieved to have it done. "Over five minutes. Our first honest-to-goodness spat."

"I know, anybody would think we were married." Graham laid his hand over hers. "It was my fault, Lee. I've been grouchy. I don't know what's the matter with me."

Lee smiled. "Could it have something to do with being tired, hungry, cold, and stressed out all in one day?"

"Don't forget scared stiff and fighting mad."

Their New York steak dinners began with mushroom-barley soup, thick and steaming, which they spooned up gratefully. The restaurant was situated atop the four-story Hilltop House Hotel, a skyscraper by Los Alamos standards, and they had been shown to a table at a huge, peaked window that must have had a spectacular view over desert and mountains during the day, but at 10 P.M. reflected only the warm, clean, comfortable wood interior of the nearly empty room back at them. By now, with the toddies and most of the soup inside them, they too were finally feeling warm and comfortable.

"Listen," Graham said, sopping up broth with a hunk of bread, "I've been thinking about what you were saying about all these people having it in for Guthrie—"

"Graham, are we sure we want to talk about this right now? Things were just starting to get pleasant again."

"We're running out of time, Lee. If Ruben doesn't have some decent leads by the time the tournament's over tomorrow, he can forget it. And I promise to be good. No more harangues." He smiled at her. "Not tonight, anyway."

"Fair enough, I guess. All right, what's on your mind?"

"What I said this afternoon when we were talking about Harrelson: there are more reasons than we know what to do with for people to hate Guthrie. Fine, some of them are worth looking into. But if Guthrie was killed because he stepped on somebody's toes too hard, then why is Boyd Marriner just as dead as he is? What does he have to do with it?"

"I know, I keep wondering about that too, and all I can

come up with is his promotion at ASN—Ted had him promoted to vice-president for golf. Do you know about that?"

"Yes, I was there when Peg called it in to Ruben." He hesitated momentarily. "Thanks, by the way. It was information we didn't have."

She shrugged. "Well, we hoped you might be able to use it," she said, trying not to show how absurdly pleased she was. "Anyway, in return, for all we know, Boyd might have promised to fire Skip once he got in." She paused while the neatly bearded, pony-tailed waiter ground pepper over their salads with a mill that could have passed for a baseball bat. "Or maybe Boyd was going to get rid of Mike Bulger; I know he didn't think much of his management style, which I can certainly understand. Or maybe Mary Ann, for that matter, or maybe—"

"Or maybe anybody at ASN. No doubt there are loads of evidence for all this."

"Not a shred," Lee admitted with a sigh.

Conversation died away while they crunched their salads, and it was not until they had had their first, soul-satisfying bites of expertly charred steak that they returned to a subject that had occupied them earlier.

"I'm still trying to make sense of what happened to us at the tower," Graham said, musing. "What in the hell was the point of that?"

"To keep us from finding the notebook, what else? I thought we agreed."

"Well, now I'm not so sure," he said, chewing energetically. "How would dumping it—and us—into the pond keep it from being found?"

"But he wasn't trying to dump us into the pond, the crud, he was trying to dump us onto those rocks."

"So? The police would still have found the notebook."

"Not if he got to it first."

198

"And how was he supposed to do that? Search through all that junk in the dark, just hoping that no one would come by and happen to notice that he'd just bulldozed a television tower over, and that our battered bodies were lying there with limbs splayed out at what the newspapers like to refer to as 'grotesque angles'?"

Lee made a face. "Would you mind not joking about our battered bodies? Anyway, he wouldn't have had to search through everything. In case you've forgotten, the notebook was in your pocket. All he had to do was get it off your body." She cut off a neat wedge of baked potato. "Your battered body."

"You're right," Graham said, "that's not funny. But the point is that he—or she, for that matter; women can drive bulldozers too, you know—he or she couldn't possibly know I had it on me, right? He'd have no idea where to look for it."

"I guess not," Lee agreed. "What then? Was he trying to—to get rid of you?"

"That'd be a pretty chancy way to get rid of someone. I don't imagine the likelihood of our getting killed would have been all that great, even if the tower had landed on the rocks. Some broken bones, maybe a cracked skull, but that'd be about all he could count on."

"But that'd be more than enough to keep you out of things through tomorrow, and maybe that's all he needed. After that, the investigation's pretty much dead. You said so yourself."

"That's a good point, but why pick on me? I don't know anything Ruben and his men don't know. Less, in fact."

"Well, what then? You're pretty good at torpedoing my theories. Let's hear one from you."

"I've been wondering," he said slowly, raising his eyes from his wine glass to meet hers, "if he might have been trying to get rid of someone else."

"Someone else?" Puzzled, she frowned at him. "*Me*? Why would anyone want to get rid of me? What did *I* do? What do *I* know?"

"I don't know, but it sure seems to me you 'happen to hear' an awful lot of things. You *have* been asking a lot of questions, haven't you?"

"Questions, me? Well, no, I wouldn't exactly say that. I—"

He held up his hands. "Relax, general amnesty, remember? No harangues. You have, haven't you?"

"Well, yes, but I wouldn't say a *lot* of questions. I did talk to one or two people for a minute or two, but I was really discreet. They'd never connect what I asked them with—"

"Who?" He had his notebook out beside his plate.

"Frank," she said. "Vern. Ummm, Harry. Oh, Bonnie."

"Christ."

"And Skip. That's it. Oh, and Mary Ann."

He was shaking his head. "Discreet is hardly the word for it," he muttered, then quickly added: "That is not to be construed as a harangue."

"Graham, even if I did ask a few questions, so what? Lots of people are asking questions. Why come after me?"

"I don't know."

"And why do it when I was with you? Why not get me alone?"

"I don't know. Maybe it's a question of time again. Maybe he was in a hurry to get you out of the way."

Lee toyed with her coffee cup. "Graham, do you really believe all this, or are you just trying to scare me into being more careful?"

He smiled. "Basically, I'm just trying to scare you into being more careful."

She laughed. "Well, it worked, let me tell you."

He leaned abruptly across the table, his clear blue eyes

luminous. His hand, which had been lying loosely over hers, tightened around her wrist. "Lee, if anything happened to you . . . I don't care whether we catch this guy or not, that doesn't matter. I just don't want anything to happen to you." His voice was thready. "I love you."

"I love you too. Very much." Her own voice had thickened as she spoke. Until tonight, it had been a long, long while since the last time they'd said those words to each other. Their unspoken rules of engagement had forbidden them, and sensible rules they were—but how sweet, how piercingly sweet, it was to say them, to hear them.

"Lee?" He fumbled with his knife and lowered his eyes, uncharacteristically shy. "About staying with me at the inn. If you don't want to—I mean, if you're not in the mood to—well, it's fine, there are two beds in the room . . ."

She smiled. What a gallant, lovely man he was, and how much he had put up with for her. And how very much indeed she did love him. She stopped his lips with a fingertip.

"One bed," she said, "will be sufficient."

Chapter 28

When Lee and Graham arrived at Peg's house the following morning, they were met in the driveway by her departing scientist-husband, Ric, already floating in his usual cloud of theoretical physics, but not so immersed that he failed to tell them that he was pretty sure his wife could be located on the back patio.

They found her standing at a portable practice tee of plastic grass, angrily swinging a golf club that kept collapsing into four hinged sections, like a folding ruler. Each time it happened Peg would mutter under her breath, consult a manual that lay open on a bench beside her, and try again, with the same result.

"Peg, what in the world is that thing?" Lee asked.

"What thing?" Peg growled, her nose in the manual.

"The thing in your hand that looks like a golf club that got run over by Amtrak."

"This," said Peg between clenched teeth, "is my so-called guaranteed-to-perform ErgoPro Dynamic Swing Trainer. A hundred and twenty-five bucks. It's supposed to cure the twelve major timing faults. If you don't do it exactly right, the stupid shaft is supposed to break down."

"Seems to be working all right," Graham observed.

Peg scowled at him and held the club out to Lee. "Here, let me see you try it."

Lee shied away. "Not on your life."

Peg was one of the legion of golf hackers, otherwise presumably intelligent people, who never-endingly sought the one trick, the single magic key, that would turn their play from duffer to decent. Lee knew better.

"Well, at least watch me," Peg said, "and tell me what I'm doing wrong."

"Sure, if I can."

Peg took her stance, stared ferociously at the perforated plastic ball she was trying to hit out onto the verge of the fairway just beyond her patio, held her breath, and pulled the club back with excruciating slowness. The joints wobbled but held. "Ha," she murmured in quiet triumph and started her downswing. The shaft wrapped itself around her shoulders like a mechanical python. She glared dolefully at Lee from within its coils.

"Well?"

"Possibly you put too much wrist into it?" Lee offered.

"No, no," Peg said impatiently. "What I'm trying to work on now is . . ." She leaned over to consult the manual. ". . . this: 'Step 5. The hips, in making their leftward rotation (preceded by a slight, lateral, nonswaying slide toward the target), pull the shoulders around in turn, communicating the centrifugal force of the powerful hip-turn first to the arms and then to the hands, *which must not uncock, however*, until the weight transfer from right to left has been accomplished by a thrusting-off motion from the inside of the right foot.' "

"It sounds simple enough," Graham said. "I don't know what your problem is."

"Yeah, just try it some time and then tell me about it. What do you think, Lee? Is that where my problem is?"

Lee laughed. "Don't ask me."

"Well, how on earth am I supposed to keep all that in mind while I'm swinging? How do *you* do it?"

"Peg, if I tried to remember all that, I wouldn't be able to hit the ball at all. You know my approach. I clear my mind, I try to relax, I step up to the ball . . . ." She shrugged. ". . . and I just hit it."

Peg had heard this from Lee more than once before. "That," she said, flinging the club away, "is disgusting. Life," she informed Graham, "is not fair."

But a moment later her round, good-natured face lit up, the unfairness of life forgotten. "Wait till you see what I have for you. Sit down at the table, the food's out. Pour yourself some coffee."

She was back in seconds, a hefty sheaf of paper in her hands. *"Avec mes compliments,"* she trumpeted, plopping it on the table in front of Graham. "Everything you ever wanted to know about Ted Guthrie."

Her mole at Grubber & Crooke had come through in a big way, with forty-five faxed pages of closely typed information on Guthrie's business and financial affairs. Peg had read through it earlier, and over a breakfast of lox, bagels, cream cheese, and scrambled eggs, they huddled head to head while she pointed out various discrepancies, omissions, and possible fishy transactions, which Graham dutifully highlighted with a marking pen.

Lee had followed along for perhaps sixty seconds, but depletion allowances, balance sheets, and asset and liability accounts were not her cup of tea, and very soon her mind was drifting. There was plenty for it to drift over. The previous two days had provided enough excitement, enough ups and downs, to last her for the next forty years. It hardly seemed possible, but at this time Friday, only forty-eight hours ago, she was riding high, leading the first High Desert Classic after one round. Graham was a thousand miles away in Carmel and as nearly out of mind as he ever got. Nobody was dead yet. She had never even heard the names of Boyd Marriner or Ted Guthrie. And now—now, my God, she had watched one of them die and unsuccessfully tried to revive the other, she had been pitched out of a tower and into a pond by a bulldozer in the dead of night, and she was a fledgling TV announcer instead of a fledgling golfer.

And she had spent the night in Graham's arms. It was mostly to this that her thoughts kept returning. Or not thoughts so much as images. Or not images so much as feelings, impossible to put into words or even to sort. By putting their relationship back on its old footing she had complicated her life immeasurably. Sex *did* complicate things, never mind the prevailing wisdom. Where she had so painfully separated and categorized the elements of her existence—golf, Graham, the present, the future—into a tidy, governable arrangement, this morning all was confusion, agitation, and indecision again.

So then why, she asked herself as if she didn't know, was she feeling anything but agitated at the moment? She was downright pleased with herself, practically purring. She felt healthy and pretty and desirable, and underneath everything else was the deeply soothing sense that, despite the calamities of the last few days, all was fundamentally right with the world.

She lathered another quarter of a bagel with cream cheese and cherry jam, topped off her coffee, and gazed with a complacent, frankly possessive pleasure at Graham. How serious, and formidable, and professional he looked, bent over a securities analysis with Peg, his unruly sandy hair brushed, his mustache groomed to military precision, his lovely, square jaw firm. She stifled a throaty chuckle; she was remembering him once or twice during the night, when

he didn't look quite so serious or so professional. Formidable, yes—

Unexpectedly, he looked up, catching Lee in full ogle.
His ready answering grin made it clear that he knew precisely what she was thinking about, and Lee, feeling herself
blush, looked quickly down at her plate.

But not quickly enough to get by Peg, who glanced
quizzically from one of them to the other. "What?"

Head down, Lee studied her bagel.

"What did I miss?" Peg insisted.

"Hmmm," Lee said, pulling over a sheet from the pile
and sinking into rapt contemplation. "A page from a loan
application. Now *this* is really interesting."

"Well, I guess nobody's going to tell me anything," Peg
said.

"It does look that way," Graham agreed. "Now explain
what's funny about this consolidated balance sheet one more
time, will you?"

Lee's face was still warm, and she kept it buried in the
application while the others got back to work. To her surprise, it did turn out to be interesting in its way. An entire
lifetime's work summarized in eighteen lines. In applying
for the loan Ted had listed the golf courses he'd redesigned;
eighteen in all. Many of the clubs were quite famous, and
she had played some of them without knowing it: Quail
Valley in California, the Breakers in Florida, Old Patriarch
in Tennessee. In each case, Ted had taken what had once
been a classic golf course in the old Scottish tradition, aus-
tere, beautiful, and devilishly challenging, with *character*
with a capital *C* leaping out at every turn—a golf course
much like Cottonwood Creek—and remade it into something between a theme park and an upscale hotel-condomin-
ium complex.

In short, a "destination resort."

They were huge income-producers for the clubs, or so

she had heard, but those who loved golf for golf's own pure, quiet sake tended to look elsewhere. No wonder the community here had been so split—

"Thanks a million, Peg," Graham said, getting to his feet. "I want to get this over to Ruben right now. If we need any more help with it, I assume you'd be game?"

"Of course, you bet. But there's something else I have to tell you. Sit down again and listen to this. You too, Lee." Portentously, she cleared her throat. "I know what the problem was between Ted Guthrie and Skip Cochrane."

"So do we," Lee said. "Ted got mad because of what Skip said on the air about his Bonnymead redesign. Bonnie Harlow told me; I just haven't had a chance to mention it to you."

"Yes, but do you know what Ted *did?*"

"Did?" Graham echoed.

"Aha, I thought this might be news to you. This is fresh off the Internet, from an attorney friend in Minneapolis who does some work for ASN. Ted actually tried to get Skip fired, how about that?"

It had happened two years earlier, when Ted, as a member of the board of directors of Meta Communications, had played an influential part in the negotiations leading to ASN's coverage of the High Desert Classic. One of Ted's early conditions had been that Skip be removed from the broadcast team. Skip's contract still had two years to run, however, and Ted had had to relent for the time being. But rumor was now rife among those who knew such things that Skip's days were numbered, that Boyd Marriner, as ASN's new vice-president for golf, had not been planning to renew his contract.

"I told you!" Lee said excitedly to Graham. "Isn't that just what I said? That gives him a motive for killing both of them!"

Peg nodded vigorously. "Exactly. I wouldn't want to tell

you how to do your job, Graham, but if I were you or Ruben, I'd be giving some serious attention to Mr. Cochrane."

"Mm."

"What does that mean?"

"It means we've already given serious attention to Mr. Cochrane. And what we found out was that at 1:51 P.M. on Friday, which is when Guthrie was electrocuted, Mr. Cochrane was—"

"On the air with Mary Ann," an abruptly deflated Lee said, "in full view of several million people. Play wasn't called until two. And even then, they just went over to the clubhouse and kept broadcasting."

Peg leaned back against her chair, arms folded. "So he's off the hook. Mary Ann too."

"That's right, but don't look so unhappy, you two," Graham said. "It was a good idea, it just didn't pan out. In any case, I'm coming around to thinking we can cross all the ASN people off our list; the folks from the WPGL too, and anybody else who's just in for the tournament. Ruben's not so sure, but I have a hunch our murderer's going to turn out to be one of your friends and neighbors, Peg. Somebody from Cottonwood Creek. Possibly a bigwig in the club."

"You don't mean a board member?" Peg asked.

"I wouldn't be surprised. Or possibly a club employee," he added as an afterthought.

"Why?" asked Lee. "Why not somebody from outside?"

"Because of what happened at the tower last night. Who-ever—"

"What tower?" asked Peg.

"—was on that bulldozer—"

"What bulldozer?" asked Peg.

"—knew just where the equipment yard was. And—"

"What equip—"

"Sorry, Peg," Graham said, "I only have a minute. Lee will fill you in after I go."

Peg sat back, mumbling away to herself. "Sure, I'm only good for *getting* information from. When it comes to *telling* me anything . . ."

"And," Graham went on to Lee, "that has to mean that he or she was thoroughly familiar with the club layout."

"I don't see how you can say that," Lee protested. "It's no secret. Anybody could find out where the equipment yard is."

"Do *you* know where it is?"

She thought for a moment. "Well, no, now that you mention it, but if I had some reason for knowing, all I'd have to do is ask somebody ahead of time."

"That's my point," Graham said. "That attack couldn't have been planned ahead of time because we had no idea we were going to be there. And it only took us five minutes to get there from the party—"

"Fifteen," Lee said. "We were kind of taking our time."

Graham smiled. "All right, fifteen. And another five in the tower before the dozer showed up. Twenty minutes in all, and whoever it was managed to get to the yard, find the dozer, get it started, and make it back to the tower. Over the cart paths. In the dark."

"Couldn't they have asked someone at the party?" Peg said, unable to stay out of it even if she couldn't quite follow along.

"Not unless they're a lot dumber than I think they are," said Graham. "You don't ask somebody where a murder weapon is and then go out and use it twenty minutes later and expect to get away with it."

"You do have a point," Lee said, "but lots of outsiders must know where the yard is. The people from ASN and the WPGL have been wandering all over this place for days. Fans too."

"And how many of them would also happen to know where the greenskeeper's shed is, and what kind of poisons are on the shelf, and what to do with those poisons?"

"And how to drive a bulldozer," Lee said.

"That too," Graham said. "But from what Ruben says, this particular variety isn't that hard if all you're doing is steering and moving it backwards and forwards. You just push and pull a couple of levers."

"Do *you* know how to drive one?"

"Well, no," Graham said with a grin. "Now that you mention it. Okay, I see your point too. Simple or not, whoever it was *knew* he could handle one or he'd never have gone to the yard in the first place."

"Exactly."

"So that's one more thing we know about him," Graham said, nodding at her as he unfolded out of his chair once more. "We might get somewhere yet. Well, I have to go." He patted the pile of papers and slipped them under his arm. "This is going to knock Ruben's eye out, Peg. You've made a friend for life there."

"Good, you never know when having the local homicide cop for a friend will come in handy."

"Especially around here," Lee said.

"I'll see myself out, Peg." Graham leaned down to kiss Lee just above the bridge of her nose. "When I'm gone you can have another cup of coffee and give Peg the details on our thrilling night together."

"*Graham!*" Lee was shocked. "I'm certainly not—I don't see how you—"

He laughed, his blue eyes crinkling in real amusement. "The *tower*," he said.

"Oh," Lee said. "Yes, well, sure."

"So what happened last night?" Peg asked, leaning forward over the table as Graham left, still laughing. "Come on; all the details."

"Well, remember when we left the party last night and didn't come back? We went to the camera tower on the fourteenth fairway to look—"

Peg flapped her hand impatiently. "I don't want to hear about the tower. I want to hear about what you *thought* he was talking about."

"The tower is a great deal more pertinent," Lee said with dignity.

"But you will tell me about the rest of it later?" Peg implored. "What else are friends for?"

Lee couldn't help smiling. "Maybe," she said. "But not *all* the details."

Chapter 29

"Get her to *say* something, for Christ's sake!" Mike Bulger's agitated voice was shouting in her left ear. Doesn't she speak English, or what?"

"Two-minutes, twenty-five . . ." said one of the assistant directors into her right ear. "Two-minutes, twenty . . ."

Lee's smile felt stuck to her face as painfully as a slab of dry ice. "Well, it was certainly a day to remember for you, Olga," she chirped bravely, "and for golf fans as well. Overcoming Susan Torresdahl's five-stroke lead took a a prodigious effort, and your incredible birdie on the final hole topped it all: a 240-yard drive, an uphill chip from a slanting lie, and then an extremely tricky 20-foot putt over the cusp of the green. But you played it perfectly. Congratulations."

She held the microphone out to Olga Gronski, the surprising come-from-behind winner of the High Desert Classic, the woman known around the WPGL, and with good reason, as the Silent Slav.

"Tanks," said Olga.

A trickle of sweat rolled down Lee's temple. "And I don't think anyone who saw it will ever forget that wonderful eagle on the twelfth hole, Olga. There you were, 210 yards from the green. Anybody else would have used a three-iron or a fairway wood to lay the ball up safely short of the bunker for a wedge shot, but you didn't settle for that, did you? You had something else in mind."

Hopefully, she held the mike out again. If her encouraging smile was any wider or any stiffer her face would crack.

"Yas," said the Silent Slav.

More anguished howls in Lee's left ear, while the countdown continued in her right. "Minute, thirty-five . . ."

"You went to your bag for the *driver*, and you went for the green—and you made it, a stunning shot that left the ball 9 feet from the pin, all ready for a makable putt."

"Dat's right," Olga agreed, and having delivered a rare two words in a row, she went whole-hog and added another. "Tanks," she said again and to Lee's horror promptly turned and left, making her way through the watching semicircle of dignitaries and officials who had assembled for the closing ceremonies, and leaving Lee staring petrified into the camera with one microphone in her hand, another at her lips, and nothing whatever to say into either of them.

Not so Mike, who blistered her ear with an explosion of bluster and panic. He had gone to great lengths earlier to impress on her that it was absolutely essential to end precisely on time; not a second earlier, not a second later. And her job at this point, her one function, was to take the broadcast to exactly five seconds before its end, when Skip would sign off by means of a voice-over, while Lee and Olga remained smiling on screen with the credits rolling over them.

Except that nobody had remembered to tell Olga.

"*Say* something!" Mike was screaming. "Talk to somebody else! Talk to somebody *else*! Human *interest*, for God's sake! *Anything* . . . !" After which he fell to incomprehensible gibbering.

"Minute, fifteen . . ." said the assistant director, whose voice was showing signs of panic as well.

So was Lee's. Her throat felt as if it were stopped up with cement. Anything sensible she might have said had fled her mind. The seventy seconds she had to fill loomed before her like seventy years. Lord, let her get out of this with her sanity intact and she'd never go near a microphone again for the rest of her life.

She licked her lips and looked wildly at the assembled dignitaries, who continued to watch amicably, unaware that the announcer before them was barely this side of catatonic and the man in charge was well on his way to the screaming meemies if not already there.

"Bonnie!" Lee croaked at the one person among them whose name she knew. "Bonnie Harlow, come over and say a few words." Not willing to chance a negative reply, she reached out, grabbed Bonnie's arm in a clawlike grasp, and plucked her from the group.

"We have Bonnie Harlow with us, ladies and gentlemen," Lee said, "one of golf's top stars in the 1980s and now field director of . . . of . . . various matters for the WPGL."

Bonnie, God bless her, understood the situation immediately and leaped expertly into the vacuum. "It's wonderful to be here, Lee. And what an exciting ending to a dramatic contest. Wasn't Olga Gronski something?"

Whew, things were looking up. Lee began to relax a little, and the two of them talked about Gronski's final charge, about Torresdahl's faltering in the clutch, about the upcoming tour schedule.

Lee pressed the right earphone to her head. Had she missed a signal? Surely it was past time to go to Skip in the announce booth.

"Forty seconds . . ." the voice said.

Good gosh, talk about time dragging. But Lee's mind

was functioning again. And with the help of a trouper like Bonnie, forty seconds would be a piece of cake.

She even had some human interest for Mike. "There must be quite a few memories here for you at this beautiful country club," she said smoothly, beginning to enjoy herself. "Your father designed it, after all. And you were here for the opening in the 1950s."

"*Please,*" Bonnie said, laughing, "the 1960s—1965, I think. And I was a *very* little girl, only about eleven. But yes, there are some very pleasant memories here."

"Nineteen sixty-five. It must have been about your father's last course."

"Actually, no, the next to last. The last one was Quail Valley in—" She faltered. Her keen, intelligent eyes fixed penetratingly on Lee's for an instant, darted away, and shot back. "—California," she finished.

The lull had lasted only a fraction of a second. It was unlikely that the television audience had even noticed it, but it had made a profound impression on Lee. In some cavern of her mind, great, unmanageable, stonelike blocks seemed to budge, then shift, then slowly slide toward one another. And finally slip into place with a *chunk* that she could almost hear.

She stared at Bonnie, her brain whirling. Quail Valley. Bonnie's father had—

"*Say* something!" Mike shouted in her ear.

"The hardware store," Lee said, her eyes locked with Bonnie's.

She could hear Mike moaning pitifully to somebody in the truck, or perhaps to the walls: "You hear that? You hear that? I tell her to say something and she says 'hardware store.' Tell me this isn't happening."

"Ten seconds . . ." said the assistant director.

Their voices scarcely registered. Lee pointed shakily at Bonnie. "You—"

"I'm sorry, I have a—I have to go," Bonnie said. She turned away with unanticipated speed, but Lee managed to clench a handful of fabric at her shoulder. With a grunt the larger woman cuffed her backhanded across the cheekbone with a bony wrist, bulling her way past as Lee stumbled to her hands and knees.

The startled watchers jumped back out of the way and Bonnie brushed by them, breaking into a run toward the larger crowd milling around the green.

"Arrest that woman!" Lee bawled from her knees, and as luck would have it Bonnie ran almost directly into a gray-haired, swag-bellied security officer who was probably too astonished and too slow-moving to get out of the way.

"Arrest that woman!" Lee shouted again, and the beefy arms of the officer closed like pincers around Bonnie. From the look of him, it had been a long time between arrests, but he held tight, lifting her to her toes before she stopped struggling and subsided.

Lee sat back on her heels, trembling and short of breath, her eyes closed. She adjusted the headset that Bonnie had knocked awry and immediately heard Mike screaming in her left ear again.

"That was *GREAT!*" he said.

Chapter 30

"Just go and *ask* her, Caitlin. She won't bite you."

This encouragement, the outcome of several minutes of tense discussion among the family of three, carried easily to the table at which Graham and Lee sat drinking bottled orange juice and watery coffee and eating egg salad sandwiches out of plastic wrappers.

Caitlin, all of twelve, bug-eyed and gangly, came up to them apprehensively and thrust out a copy of the *Los Alamos Monitor* with one hand and a well-chewed ballpoint pen with the other.

"Could I please have your autograph?"

This was far from an everyday phenomenon, but it had happened before. "Sure," Lee said with a smile, taking the paper and turning it right side up.

ARREST THAT WOMAN!!! the front-page headline screamed in fat black letters. Underneath it was a photograph of an open-mouthed Lee floundering on her hands and knees, doing a first-rate imitation of a constitutionally ungainly bird dog.

She put her hand over her mouth, trying to keep from giggling. "Oh, dear."

"You're laughing about it, anyhow," Graham said. "That's an improvement."

He was referring to her reaction the previous night when they had gotten back to the lodge after a three-hour session at the police station with Ruben and the Los Alamos district attorney. Graham had turned on the television set just as CNN's *Sports Tonight* ran a clip of the scuffle between Bonnie and Lee—twice, the second time in slow motion. Unaccountably, in a strange, mixed flood of relief and depression, she had been unable to look at it. She had made Graham turn it off and had fallen heavily asleep not long afterward.

She had slept deeply, awakening in the morning cheerier and more relaxed, with the sense of a great weight lifted from her. She was due again at the police station in the afternoon to review her statement, but at Graham's suggestion they had decided on a morning change of scene, driving south on State Road 4 to the famous pueblo ruins at Bandelier National Monument. Having neglected to get themselves breakfast on the way, they had made their first stop the snack bar at the visitor center, where Lee had been spotted by Caitlin and her almost equally excited parents.

"To Caitlin," she wrote beside the photo. "With best wishes, Lee Ofsted."

The girl snatched it back and turned hopefully to Graham. "Are you anybody?"

"Me? No, I'm not anybody," Graham said. "Sorry," he added apologetically when the girl's face fell.

"Oh, that's all right," Caitlin said civilly. "It's not your fault." She went back to her beaming parents hugging the newspaper to her bosom.

"I guess you're famous again, huh?" Graham said.

Lee smiled. "You bet. All day Monday."

When the other people in the snack bar who had witnessed this began to eye her, Lee and Graham exchanged a glance, gathered up what was left of their breakfasts and took them outside to an isolated corner of the tree-shaded picnic area. For a couple of minutes they ate quietly, setting an occasional crumb at the edge of the table for a venturesome jay or tossing one on the ground for the shy, peeping nuthatches that flitted through the foliage. Six feet from them Frijoles Creek, sparkling and clear, purled over its smooth bed of pebbles.

"Up to answering a few questions?" Graham asked after a while. "There are a few things I'm not too clear on."

"About yesterday? About Bonnie?"

He nodded.

"If I can. It's—it hardly seems real to me. Like something I saw on television."

"It's real, all right. About six million people *did* see it on television."

"Don't remind me." She shook out the sandwich wrapping so that the last morsels fell to the nuthatches. "All right, what aren't you clear about?"

"About how you knew it was Bonnie."

She frowned at him. "But I explained that to Ruben. In excruciating detail. You were there."

"Explain it again. Please."

She sighed. "I already knew Bonnie's father had been the original architect for Cottonwood Creek," she told him almost by rote. "And when she mentioned that he also did Quail Valley, I remembered that Ted Guthrie had redesigned that one too, a few years ago. I saw it on that loan application. So the rest of it—well, it sort of came to me in a flash."

"Don't forget to tell that to the jury when they call you."

"But it's the truth. I suddenly realized she had a motive for killing him. From her point of view he'd already ruined one of her father's designs—well, from mine too—and now here he was getting ready to desecrate another. What if she was trying to protect his memory, his legacy? What if she thought the only way to do that was to kill Ted? What if—"

"That's an awful lot of what-ifs," Graham said.

"But she knew that once Ted was dead the whole project would die too; not only was he the force behind it, he was going to do all the work for nothing as part of the arrangement. They'd have to come up with the money for someone else. And even if they ever did put it together again, at the very least *he* wouldn't be the architect. And that was important to her. Remember, Quail Valley wasn't the only one of Harlow's courses that Ted had changed completely. He'd also redesigned Oak Hollow in the 1970s. This would have been the third time he took one of her father's classic courses and cutesied it to death. From Bonnie's point of view, of course."

Graham looked doubtful. "I know, but—"

"Ray Harlow was one of the very best of his day, Graham. He was supposed to go down in history, like George Crump or Robert Trent Jones. But now it turns out that only one of his original designs is still around: Cottonwood Creek. Period. All the rest have been 'revitalized' somewhere along the line."

"Yes, but—"

"And if Cottonwood went the same way, there would have been nothing left of Ray Harlow at all; no memorial, no example of his work. Bonnie felt she couldn't let that happen, especially not at the hands of someone who'd practically made a career out of—of ravaging her father's courses."

"I know, but . . . ."

She waited. "But what?"

"You mean I can speak now?"

"Don't be funny. But what? And are you planning on unwrapping that cookie or not?"

Graham pulled the plastic from a Frisbee-sized chocolate chip cookie and put it on the table between them. "There are a couple of things that are bothering me; maybe they don't amount to much, but they bother me. First, I keep wondering how the heck someone like Bonnie Harlow would know what she had to know about high-voltage wires, let alone how to handle a bulldozer the way she did. I mean, she's been a golfer or a golf official all her life."

"That's easy," Lee said. "She learned it from her father."

"Her *father*? He was an architect."

"He was a *golf course* architect. These aren't people who sit around in shirtsleeves over a drawing board. Creating a golf course is like sculpting this huge piece of land. The architect's right there all the time and he better know everything there is to know about earthmoving machinery. If Bonnie tagged along after her dad when she was a kid, she'd be bound to know about it too. I used to talk my father into letting me run his cement mixer, so why not a bulldozer in her case?"

Graham thought it over. "Possible," he said. "And high-voltage lines?"

Lee munched some cookie. "A fact of life on any course that's designed around a community. The architect has to put in a corridor for electricity and then work with the power company to install the lines, or at least he did before underground wiring."

"Mm."

"You said there was something else bothering you."

Graham took a moment to get his thoughts together. "I'm not arguing with you here. Everything you said before—Cottonwood Creek's being Harlow's only remaining course, Ted Guthrie's having already redesigned *two* of Harlow's earlier courses—is stuff we've found out since Bonnie was arrested. What I want to know is how you knew Bonnie was the killer *yesterday*."

Lee broke off another piece and chewed it slowly. "She looked funny when she mentioned Quail Valley, as if she thought she might have given something away."

"I've seen the tape. It was just a little pause. She didn't look funny to me. Not to Ruben either."

Lee shrugged. "Well, she did to me. She looked guilty."

Wonderingly, Graham shook his head. "And that made you think about the hardware store?"

"That made me think about Ted. And that made me think about Boyd. And *that* made me think about the hardware store."

Except that "think" wasn't exactly the right word. She didn't remember doing anything remotely like thinking. One second she was as much in the dark as ever; the next it was as if she suddenly understood, but didn't know what it was she understood; and the next, everything was crystal-clear. Her mind had jumped back two days, to when Boyd had been explaining Lou's new job to him and talking about visiting the hardware store. He had seen Bonnie there the previous night, he'd said; he'd seen her there buying a whole—

A whole what? He'd never gotten to finish because Bonnie had jumped in with some inconsequential remark about not revealing a woman's secrets. It had seemed silly to Lee at the time. What was there to buy in a True Value store to be embarrassed about? But of course Bonnie had always been a bit of an oddball, and Lee had promptly forgotten all about it. Until that moment, as she stood there with the microphone in her hand.

And then it had seemed anything but inconsequential. What if the reason Bonnie had cut him off was because she was afraid he was going to say that he had seen her with a newly purchased sixty-foot coil of wire? What if (Graham certainly had a point about there being a lot of what-ifs) she had later killed him to prevent him from talking about it to the police?

At which point Lee had impulsively blurted: "The hardware store," and the excitement had started.

"But you didn't *know* any of that," Graham insisted. "What if you were wrong?"

"Why would she have turned tail and run if I was wrong?"

"She didn't turn tail and run. She said she had another appointment or something and started to leave. Whereupon you tackled her—out of the blue—like a linebacker going after a quarterback. That was when she started to run. I probably would have run too."

"All the same," Lee said complacently, "I was right. I think you and Ruben just have your noses out of joint because I figured it out before you did."

"Oh, hell—" Graham began crossly, but then broke into his easy smile. "You know, you just might have a point there."

Pensively, Lee rolled a doughy ball of cookie between her fingers. "What will happen to her, Graham?"

"Who knows? Her lawyer's made it clear she's not about to confess to anything. She'll go to trial and we'll see. The evidence is all circumstantial, and these days anything can happen."

She looked up sharply. "Circumstantial? What about the wire? We can prove she bought it."

This had come about as the result of some quick work by Ruben the night before and early this morning. He had compared the cut end of the wire that had been found near the cart path to the cut end of the roll of identical wire that was in the True Value store on Diamond Drive and been assured by a metals specialist from the national lab that they matched beyond any possibility of doubt. Moreover, store records showed that the wire had been purchased Thursday night, the night before Ted's death, when Boyd had also made his purchases.

And most significant of all, the clerk who had been on duty remembered Bonnie clearly. Number two triplex aluminum wire was electrician's wire, he'd said, and he'd never seen an electrician who looked anything like the lady who bought it. He'd unhesitatingly identified her from a set of photos.

"We can prove she bought the wire," Graham said, "but we can't prove she used it. So it's circumstantial. So is everything else." He smiled. "Or should I say 'inferential'?"

Lee laughed. Last night Mr. Avila, the district attorney, a dour, exacting man with ears as droopy as a beagle's, had irritated not only Lee but Ruben and Graham as well. He had contributed little to the hour-long deliberation that followed Lee's formal deposition, other than interrupting their train of thought with one "Why?" after another.

And then responding to whatever they said with a single contemptuous word: "Inferential."

Why, he had wanted to know, would an intelligent woman like Bonnie have been careless enough (a) to buy the wire in a local hardware store, and (b) to simply throw it away beside the cart path afterward, where it could have been and indeed was so easily found?

Because, Ruben suggested, she never expected anyone to think Guthrie's murder was anything but what it seemed: accidental death by lightning.

"Inferential," sniffed Mr. Avila.

And why, if Bonnie was so worried about Boyd's telling the police he'd seen her with the wire, did she wait until the following day to get rid of him instead of disposing of him at once?

For the same reason, said Graham: she never thought that anyone would suspect foul play, let alone grasp how it was done. But when the police began showing interest—specifically, when Ruben came to the caddie yard looking for Lee on Friday evening—she began to worry that they were on to something. And if the murder method were to become public knowledge, Boyd would surely remember having seen her with the wire. The next morning he was dead.

Mr. Avila pursed his lips dismissively. "Inferential."

And why would Bonnie (who even Mr. Avila agreed might know something about earthmoving equipment as a result of her father's profession) climb into a bulldozer and attack Lee and Graham in the camera tower? With Boyd already dead, what was so important about the notebook?

But it wasn't the notebook, Lee said, it was Lee herself who was the object. Bonnie knew Lee was prying into things, finding one pretext or another to ask people (including Bonnie, as it happened) all sorts of questions about Ted Guthrie and his relationships. She also knew that Lee had heard Boyd mention having met her at the hardware store. How long would it be before it occurred to the meddlesome Lee that hardware stores were where you bought wire and she mentioned it to Graham, if not to Ruben? So she had to be given something else to occupy her, at least for the rest of the weekend, after which it would all become ancient history. And a broken bone or two would do that nicely.

This time there was a pause before Mr. Avila spoke.

"Inferential," he said.

Ruben had finally exploded, hammering on the briefing room table with exasperation. "Dammit, Jesse, who the hell's side are you on? If you don't want to indict, just say so and let's all get out of here and go home! You want her to walk? Fine, who cares, what's one more murderer on the streets?"

Mr. Avila studied Ruben with narrowed eyes, slowly stroking his long, blue-black jaw.

If he says "inferential," Lee thought, I'm going to strangle him myself. Right here in the police station.

But he had surprised them. "No one ever said you couldn't convict, let alone indict, on inferential evidence," he'd said, accompanying the words with his first smile of the evening, not an appealing sight. "I say we've got a case, Detective."

"Inferential, circumstantial, whatever," Lee said now to Graham, "I hope she gets what's coming to her."

"I think we can assume Avila and Ruben will do a good job. You probably *will* be called, you know."

"I know. I'm not looking forward to it."

She had a sudden, bittersweet image of a smiling, open-faced Boyd offering her the broadcasting job within hours of her having to drop out of the tournament. And of Bonnie Harlow standing beside him at the time, so very friendly and supportive.

"Or maybe I am," she said.

She drained her coffee and looked doubtfully at the sizable segment of cookie that remained. "I can't handle any more chocolate chips. Or any more talk about Bonnie. How about seeing the sights?"

For almost an hour they walked, saying little, following the visitor paths but paying scant attention to the guidebook they'd bought. They walked through groves of whispering cottonwood trees, and along the base of sheer, towering, timeless cliffs, and among the collapsed, silent ruins of sprawling pueblos whose heyday had come and gone long before the first Europeans had arrived. When the path rose they followed it through weather-sculpted rock passageways to a line of ancient cliff dwellings: small, square caves carved out of the soft volcanic tuff a dozen feet above them, three or four of them reachable by sturdy pinyon ladders that had been propped invitingly against the cliff face.

Lee grasped a ladder rung. "Come on, let's have a look."

Graham looked doubtfully up at the opening. "I don't

know about this. The last time I went up a ladder with you . . ."

She laughed and clambered up. When Graham climbed up after her, they found themselves in a rough-cut cave no more than ten feet deep, the only indication of human habitation a soot-blackened ceiling, whether from modern or ancient fires they had no way of knowing.

Graham stood looking out over Frijoles Canyon. "Nice view. Let's sit down for a while." He dropped down at the cave entrance, his feet hanging over the edge, and made room for Lee. She sat next to him, overlooking almost the whole of the narrow, winding canyon. They could see Frijoles Creek itself, coppery with reflected light from the reddish cliffs, and a few groups of people moving slowly along the paths from ruin to ruin.

"Well," Graham said and looked expectantly at her.

Her chest tightened. This was it. The Talk.

She'd felt it coming on while they were walking; twice he'd begun to speak, but changed his mind. She was terrified. With all the thought she'd given to it, she still didn't know what she would say if he asked her to marry him. If she really, truly felt that she would lose him if she said no, then she would say yes. She would give up the tour. Maybe learn the business end of golf, become a club pro, and settle in at one of the multitude of courses around Carmel. There were a lot worse ways to end up. She would do it with a failing heart, but she had no choice, because without Graham . . .

"Well," she replied.

He smiled at her. "Get ready, this is going to come as a surprise."

Somehow, she didn't think so. She tried to smile back. "Oh?"

His grin broadened. He looked happy and excited, bringing Lee a stab of guilt at her own wretched shilly-shallying. What kind of a woman was she to be in a fearful, cold sweat because a terrific man like Graham was going to propose?

He lifted the breast-pocket flap of his denim jacket and reached inside with two fingers.

A ring, she thought. He's already gone and bought a ring. Here it comes, the Moment of Truth.

"I'm going into business," he announced, producing a cream-colored business card.

"You're—" She stared uncomprehendingly at him for a moment, then dissolved into helpless laughter.

"Thank you for your confidence," Graham said.

"I'm sorry." She couldn't stop laughing. "It's just that it really is a surprise. I thought—I thought—"

"I know what you thought. Read the card."

She took it from his hand. "COUNTERMEASURE, INC.," was printed in handsomely embossed letters. "Consultants in Personal and Corporate Security. Graham T. Sheldon, President."

Lee looked up at him and shook her head. "I don't understand."

There wasn't much to understand, Graham told her. He was quitting Carmel PD—he had given them six weeks' notice three weeks ago—and starting his own consulting firm. He had already hired three as-needed employees and was looking for another. And the business was off and running, with three clients already signed up: a Mexico City bank that wanted training for their executives in how to deflect kidnapping attempts; a private Texas college that had hired him to develop a system to guard against letter bombs; and . . .

"*And,*" Graham said, looking mightily pleased with himself, "an assignment—a well-paying assignment—to come up with an ongoing plan to beef up public security for—hold on to your hat—the Women's Professional Golf League."

"WPGL? I still don't understand. What—why—"

"I sent them a proposal months ago. I've been out to Fort Lauderdale twice to talk to them, and last week they finally went for it."

"But we already have security guards."

"I'm not talking about a few guards monitoring the entrances so nobody gets in without a ticket," he said scornfully, "I'm talking about a strategy, a set of contingency plans, a system. With tennis stars getting stabbed and ice skaters hiring hit men to cripple the competition, things have gotten scary out there. Who knows, I might even specialize in sports organizations."

Her mind was still whirling. "Yes, but what about your police work, your career?"

He passed the question off with a careless shrug. "Lee, don't you realize what this means? As of next month, I'm practically as transient as you are. I make my own schedule, I can get out of Carmel whenever I want; I can even afford it. And—is this a master stroke, or what?—the terms of the WPGL contract require me—*require* me—to be on site for at least eight tour events during the next year; more if it seems advisable. We could see each other practically every week if we wanted to." He paused. "Assuming you didn't mind my chasing you around the country."

What he was telling her was getting through at last. If she was willing to take the risks of involvement and complication that went along with seeing him more often, then he was willing to suspend indefinitely his need for marriage, a family, a stable life—all the things they had never once talked about but that had been standing between them like a wall all the same. And he had proven it by discarding his own solid and fulfilling career like a worn-out raincoat.

Because despite that offhanded shrug, she knew that it had been far from easy for him. Graham was one of those rare policemen who found real satisfaction in what they did; he loved putting the bad guys away. And that was something that consultants couldn't get to do much of.

Well, she was willing, all right. She was more than willing, she was tingling with excitement. Talk about having the best of both worlds; she would have golf and Graham too. It was too perfect; more than she deserved.

"It's all right with me," she said huskily. "In fact, it just may be the best offer I've had all morning."

He laughed. "See, I told you you'd like it."

"And after a while—after a year or two, we can think about—about—"

He brushed her comments aside. "Oh, I'll trust you to make an honest man of me someday. In the meantime this'll do just fine. Let's walk some more."

He got to his feet, brushed the dirt from his jeans, and pulled her up.

At the bottom of the ladder she stopped him with a hand on his arm. "Graham," she said, "have you given any thought to the downside to all this?"

"What downside?"

"You might have to learn something about golf."

He laid his hand on his heart. "Good Lord, let's hope it doesn't come to that."